THE SEVEN STAIR CREW
STREET KINGS

BRAD V. COWAN

LORIMER

James Lorimer & Company Ltd., Publishers
Toronto

James Lorimer & Company Ltd., Publishers acknowledges the support of the Ontario Arts Council. We acknowledge the financial support of the Government of Canada through the Canada Book Fund for our publishing activities. We acknowledge the support of the Canada Council for the Arts which last year invested $24.3 million in writing and publishing throughout Canada. We acknowledge the Government of Ontario through the Ontario Media Development Corporation's Ontario Book Initiative.

Book design: Meghan Collins

Library and Archives Canada Cataloguing in Publication

Cowan, Brad V.
Street kings / Brad V. Cowan.

(The Seven Stair Crew)
Issued also in electronic format.
ISBN 978-1-4594-0451-9 (bound).--ISBN 978-1-4594-0450-2 (pbk.)

I. Title. II. Series: Cowan, Brad V. Seven Stair Crew.

PS8605.O924S87   2013   jC813'.6   C2012-908243-0

James Lorimer & Company Ltd.,
Publishers
317 Adelaide Street West,
Suite #1002
Toronto, ON, Canada
M5V 1P9
www.lorimer.ca

Distributed in the United States by:
Orca Book Publishers
P.O. Box 468
Custer, WA U.S.A.
98240-0468

Printed and bound in Canada
Manufactured by Friesens Corporation in Altona, Manitoba,
Canada in February 2013
Job # 81641

For Michael Cowan

The Seven Stairs * Plaza

© Gale Finch

MAIN ST.

Main Street of Drayton

Dress Shop

Sandwich Shop

hubba

fountain

planters

RJ's Dads office (real estate)

To "the courtyard"

benches

The Seven Stairs

Mailbox

Concrete bench

Concrete bench

garbage

Parking Lot

CHAPTER 1
THE CREW

Cale Finch popped a perfect frontside one-eighty ollie down the three stairs at the front of Allenside Elementary School, rolled toward the low curb, and set up for a switch pop shove-it. He bent his knees, cracked the nose of his board against the concrete, and let it rise and spin before he caught it back on his feet, landing perfectly and rolling away clean. It was Friday afternoon and spring break had just begun. Although it was only mid-March, the weather was getting milder, and that meant Cale could finally get back to doing what he loved best: skateboarding.

He rolled down the hill toward the main street of Drayton, population twenty-five thousand. He knew his friends would be waiting for him in the plaza beside the Seven Stairs. They were in Drayton Junior High and school let out fifteen minutes earlier for them.

There were four skaters that Cale hung out with, and as he pushed his board closer and closer to the centre of town, he pictured each of them in his head. He imagined that Josh, the skinny, quiet one, would be fiddling with an old camcorder, cleaning the lens and humming quietly to himself. He pictured Ryan, the jokester, doing dorky skate tricks and making his famous monkey face to random people passing by. Skylar would probably have a fresh pair of shoes and a new deck, and he'd be practising an incredibly technical trick on it.

Cale's speed increased as he reached the steepest part of the hill and the fresh March wind hit his throat. He took a deep breath. That's when he thought of JT, the oldest in the group. He was without a doubt the best skater of the bunch, which also made him the most intimidating — at least to Cale.

The group called themselves the Seven Stair Crew or SSC for short. Cale wasn't officially a member, but they let him hang out with them. He tried to tell himself that he didn't really understand the difference, but deep down inside, he knew the reason he wasn't a real member. It wasn't the fact that he was twelve and the rest of them were thirteen (except for JT, who had just turned fourteen). It wasn't his skating style, either — JT had told Cale that he was "stoked on his relaxed skating style."

The one thing that held him back, the thing he rolled around in his head every night before he fell asleep, was this: he had not ollied down the seven stairs that gave the Seven Stair Crew its name.

The seven stairs were not an obstacle that the guys skated every day. They were reserved for special occasions. Sure, every so often, JT would call out, "I'm gonna hardflip the Seven," or Skylar would attempt to bust a kickflip down them for fun, but the stairs themselves were super-gnarly. First, there was a crack in the concrete right near the top step, which meant that a skater's ollie had to be a bit earlier than normal. Next, the actual stairs ran longer than normal. Then there was the landing, the sketchiest part of all. The ground was smooth with newly laid asphalt, but even if a skater did snap a perfect ollie with enough speed to carry him, he would land on a pretty busy back street and cars were very often parked in the run-out. The Seven Stair Crew always posted a lookout at the bottom of the Seven to call out "Clear!" if there were no cars or people coming. But there was always a chance that right when one of the dudes was rolling toward that crack at the top step, psyching himself up and ready to pop his tail at the perfect instant, the lookout would yell "Car!" and he'd have to bail out.

Ollieing these seven treacherous stairs was the

secret initiation into the Seven Stair Crew. Cale had tried once with disastrous results, and he'd been a bit freaked out at the thought of attempting it ever since. Today was different, though. He was ready to give the stairs another shot. He pumped his leg harder and felt the spring air whiz by his face. As he cracked a speedy switch one-eighty over a sewer grate, he told himself, *Today's the day, Cale, today's the day*.

Cale snapped an ollie up the curb and into the open-air mini-mall that was home to the Top Slice sandwich shop, a ladies' clothing store called Valcienna, a real estate office, and the Seven Stairs. Drayton didn't have many good spots to skate but the mini-mall was the exception. It had a few ledges in the main plaza, a perfect set of four stairs, and a couple of concrete benches on the lead-up to the Seven Stairs — overall great variety in terrain and obstacles. What made the plaza even better was that Ry's dad worked out of the real estate office. The shopkeepers all liked and respected Ry's dad, and since he didn't have a problem with his son and his friends hanging out there, neither did they. Provided that a flying skateboard didn't destroy a window, the Seven Stair Crew was cool to skate there.

Cale rode up to three of the guys sitting in the shade on one of the long concrete benches. Josh wasn't fiddling with his camera, Skylar wasn't spinning his board in some new flip-trick variation, and Ryan was nowhere to be seen. Instead, Josh, Skylar, and JT were staring silently at a yellow piece of paper.

"What's up, guys? Where's Ry?" Cale said quietly, sliding to a stop.

"He went to Florida for the week with his parents," said Skylar.

"Yeah, he's gonna be mad he didn't have time to practice for this!" said JT, thrusting the yellow piece of paper toward Cale.

Cale looked at the page in his hand. It read:

"ARE YOU A STREET KING?"

THEN ENTER THE

KING'S COURT SPRING SKATE CONTEST

SATURDAY, MARCH 14 AT 11 A.M.

STREET COURSE BEST RUN

MINI-RAMP CONTEST

$8 ENTRANCE FEE, CASH PRIZES!
BBQ LUNCH!

"This is at Toby's place, huh?" Cale said, recognizing the address. "He was talking about this last time I saw him."

"Toby is such a poser, man. Even with all the ramps his dad builds, he still sucks," JT said, which made Skylar laugh a little.

JT snapped the page back from him. "You gonna enter it, Cale?"

Cale suddenly felt like he'd done something wrong. JT had put him on the spot and Cale had no idea how to answer him.

"Um, I'm not sure," was all Cale could get out.

Toby was in the same grade as Cale at Allenside Elementary. He wasn't a very good skater, but he was a nice kid, and Cale always tried to be cool to him. He felt like speaking up in Toby's defence, but fearing he'd make himself a target, he shut his mouth and tried not to move. Even if he did speak up, he was sure it would come out all wrong.

"You should totally enter the contest, Cale," Josh said, picking up his old Mini-DV camcorder. Josh rarely spoke, but when he did, his words carried weight. Cale thought about it. It was exactly one week and one day from today, so he didn't have to make up his mind immediately.

"Maybe, but I dunno, man," Cale said, trying to

act cool about the whole thing. "I thought today I'd try the Seven again."

The mood in the plaza lifted. Skylar put down his iced tea and rose to his feet. "Whoa! Alright!" he hooted. "Josh has got the video camera and everything!"

Cale spun his board under his feet and looked at JT, who had the final say. JT just shrugged his shoulders. "He can try it, but it doesn't count if Ry's not here. All four of us have to witness it. That's the way it works."

Skylar sat back down and ran his fingers through his shaggy blond hair. "Oh man! Come on, he'll nail it this time. He got so close last time!" he pleaded.

Skylar was being a bit generous. "Don't remind me," said Cale, rubbing his butt and thinking back to that day last November when he'd tried it. It had been cold enough to see his own breath, if the wind hadn't whipped it away as soon as it came out. Cale, in his jean jacket and knit cap, had been practising kickflip backside tailslides on one of the ledges. When he landed one perfectly, those watching shouted "Yeah!" so loud that it had echoed against the low-ceilinged part of the plaza. JT had rolled by Cale, slapped him a high-five, and said casually, "Today would be a perfect day to try the Seven, dude."

That's all it had taken. In an instant, the boys had taken up their positions: Ry standing at the bottom of the stairs as lookout, Josh and Skylar perching on their tiptoes on the second bench to get the best view, and JT standing right beside Cale at the top of the run-up. "You got this, man. Don't even think twice," JT had said.

Cale had nodded knowingly, hoping that acceptance into the Seven Stair Crew was merely moments away. Ry had given the all-clear from the distance. Cale had cranked his right leg — he rode goofy — and rolled with speed toward the stairs. He had felt his heart pumping faster and faster and the harsh wind whipping by his face. As he looked down at a small chip in his board, he lost his concentration and a very small shred of doubt in his mind began to chatter, a little voice telling him that he wouldn't make it, he couldn't make it, that something was about to go wrong. That little voice had been right.

Cale remembered the actual attempt in great detail. He smacked his tail on the ground but not quite hard enough. As he drifted through the air, dropping rapidly, everything moved in slow motion. Not only because he realized that his ollie wasn't big enough, but also because, in the split second of his liftoff, Ry called out the dreaded word, "Car!"

Then the loudest voice in Cale's head had been the one that screamed, "Bail out!"

He kicked his skateboard away from his feet, landed on the bottom step with the heel of his left foot, and then rolled onto the street. He skidded across the pavement and came to a jolting stop directly in the path of the oncoming car.

The car ground to a halt about five feet away. A bald guy in a trench coat jumped out yelling, "What the hell is wrong with you, kid?! I could have killed you!"

All Cale could think about was the searing pain in his rear and shooting up his back. It had felt like his whole side had been raked over hot coals.

But that was four months ago. Cale now had a brand new set-up, which meant new everything — deck, wheels, trucks, bolts, and new grip tape, all paid for by snow shovelling. Cale had also grown an inch or two over the winter and had been practising long-distance ollies in the parking garage at the end of his street. So here he was, ready to tackle the Seven Stairs again, and JT was putting a stop to the whole thing.

Unbelievable! Cale thought, but he kept his mouth shut. There is no way he would defy JT. Instead, he looked at the ground, unblinking.

Josh, who was still fiddling with the video

camera's battery, broke the silence. "If I shoot video of Cale landing it and we can show Ry when he gets back, then he'd be witnessing it, right?" Josh asked. He didn't look up, but everybody knew the question was directed at JT.

JT looked like he was rolling the question around in his head. He looked up at the bright sky after a few long seconds and said, "Okay."

CHAPTER 2
THE SEVEN

Cale swept the landing area at the bottom of the steps with his foot. Skating in the spring in Drayton was always a bit dodgy. When the snow melted, it left behind little pockets of sand and pebbles, like tiny rocks that stopped skateboard wheels in their tracks. Digging the pebbles out of wounds was like jabbing them with a red-hot poker.

When Cale was confident the asphalt was clean, he darted up the Seven Stairs and stared down them one final time. He closed his eyes, took a deep breath, and visualized himself landing softly, knees bent to absorb the shock, and rolling away clean.

Josh set himself up at the bottom of the stairs, picking the best angle to film from, with JT standing right beside him. Skylar was lookout and nervously snapped his head left, then right, getting a feel for oncoming cars or people.

Cale set up a bit further back than he had the last time he tried the stairs. *The more speed, the better*, he thought.

"All clear, bro!" Skylar called out, and Cale began to push.

A rush of adrenaline surged through Cale's body and he put his all into every movement his body made. He had a ton of speed and felt the stairs rushing toward him as if he were being pulled by some huge river's current. He snapped his tail and popped a perfect, incredibly high ollie. Then he sucked up his legs and the board rose with him. He reached the pinnacle of the ollie, cradled the board with his feet, and effortlessly touched down on the smooth asphalt at the bottom.

He had conquered the Seven Stairs!

He rolled to the opposite side of the street and raised his hands in the air — not out of victory but out of sheer surprise.

Skylar yelped. He jogged toward Cale, gave him a high-five, and threw his arm around Cale's neck. "That was sick, bro! Your ollie was so huge!"

Cale was all smiles as he popped his board into his hand and walked back across the road toward where Josh had been filming. JT was smiling, but Cale could see there was something hidden under the smile. "You nailed it, man," JT said, raising his fist up and pounding it against Cale's.

Cale was panting a bit, and he leaned on his knee to catch his breath. Josh still hadn't said anything.

"How'd it look on camera?" Cale asked, picking at the torn suede surrounding the ollie hole in his right shoe. He could feel his sock poking through.

Josh looked at the ground, looked at JT, and then looked toward Cale. "Sorry, man," he said, "the battery died."

Cale couldn't believe it. "You mean, like, you can't play it back? Or you mean it didn't work the whole time?"

JT answered. "He got you rolling up, but it died just before you ollied."

Josh just shook his head. "Sorry, man," he said again.

Cale knew the video camera was temperamental. It was a junky old thing that Josh had bought at a pawnshop for forty bucks, so not much was to be expected. Still, Cale's heart sank. After having conquered the Seven Stairs, there was no proof to show Ry when he came back from Florida, no evidence that Cale had ollied it perfectly. Most importantly, there was no way he was going to be in the SSC unless he ollied the stairs again.

★　　★　　★

Are You a Street King? That's all Cale could think of as he piloted his board toward home. He wasn't even sure what it meant. A car honked loudly as it passed Cale, sending him off balance. He stepped awkwardly off his deck as his wheels hit a rough patch. He managed to steer his board back to the smoother pavement, but a shiver shot through him as the car whooshed by. He shook his head and his heart pounded in the wake of the near-bail.

I'm definitely not a street king, he thought. *I'm more like a street fool.*

Cale rounded the corner of Simmons Crescent and saw the porch light of his townhouse was on. All of the houses on his street looked the same: two-storey, brown brick houses packed together like a row of squished faces with garage doors for yawing mouths. Cale's kitchen window had a little butterfly suction-cupped to it, the garage door had a few black spots from the tennis balls he used to throw at it, and the curb out front had grind marks on it. These little details didn't make his house any nicer, but they made it *his*. So did the porch light, which Mom left on until Cale got home.

He smiled, thinking of his mom inside. *I've got to tell her about my ollie down the Seven,* he thought, as he popped over a crack at the bottom of the driveway and kicked his board into his hand. He was excited as he jogged up the stairs toward the door, but just before he entered, he remembered the botched video. The thought of having to ollie those stairs again sent a freezing jolt through his spine. *Maybe I won't tell her*, he though, letting the door slam behind him as he went inside.

"Cale, is that you?" his mom called up from the basement. "There's a voicemail from the skateboard shop for ya, honey."

Cale dashed to the phone, punched in the voicemail number, and let out a sigh at what he heard. "Hey, Cale, it's Mark from Drayton Skates. Got your new kicks in, buddy! They look pretty tight! They were actually five bucks less than you paid, so I've even got a bit of change for ya! I'm closing up shop now, but come in tomorrow to pick them up. We're open eleven to six." There was a pause, then he continued, "Hey, I don't know if you heard, but Russ Hammond and his son Toby are holding a contest next Saturday. It'd be really good to see you in it, man. Alright, peace."

Cale leaned against the counter in the kitchen. He had no idea that Mark Skinner might urge him to sign up for the contest. At seventeen years old, Mark was by far the best skater in Drayton, and Cale had looked up to him ever since he started skating three years ago. Mark was more than just a local legend. He was a supportive older skater who looked out for all the younger kids and was even spearheading a plan to get Drayton to build a new skate park.

Cale's mom leaned into the kitchen. "That's kind of a cool message, huh?" she said.

Cale just tried to shrug it off. He reached into the fridge, grabbed the bottle of orange juice, and drank right from the container.

"Why don't you use a glass, mister?" said his mom, but Cale knew she didn't really mind. She was cool that way. His mom spent most of her time in her basement studio, painting things like a half an apple with its seeds and droplets of juice or the very centres of flowers. She sold the huge canvases to fancy restaurants or health spas in hotels. Once she received a commission to paint a large mural in a café downtown in the big city a half-hour from Drayton. When she had finished, she took Cale to see her work. She had painted all sorts of different people chatting away in a sidewalk café in the springtime, and the details were so real that at first glance, it looked like a photograph. Cale had felt proud as he sat under his mother's mural drinking his milkshake at the café.

That had almost made up for the times that Cale's mom went weeks without selling a painting.

She always came up with a way of making ends meet. Cale did his part, too, working at odd jobs so that he could buy new skateboards or skate shoes or videos. If he didn't have a goal, he'd simply hide his savings in his room, in a phone he'd taken the working parts out of and turned into his personal piggy bank. There wasn't much in there now — after paying for his new shoes and with the snow gone and the grass not ready to cut — only twenty-eight bucks.

"What's this contest Mark's talking about?" Mom asked as Cale slid the juice back into the fridge.

"I dunno, just this thing Toby and his dad are doing," Cale answered, trying to avoid the subject.

"You think you'll enter?" she asked.

"Probably not. Whatever. I dunno," he said.

As Cale ducked past his mom on the way out of the kitchen, she grabbed him and gave him a quick kiss on the top of his head. "Dinner's in half an hour, okay kiddo?"

Cale thumped up the stairs and headed to his room to read the new issue of *Sequence*, his favourite skate magazine. Halfway to his room he thought again of telling his mom about the Seven Stair ollie but decided to keep it to himself.

CHAPTER 3
KING'S COURT

It was Saturday and Cale was sitting on the smooth white carpet in Skylar's massive basement with Josh and JT. Skylar's house was huge. He always had a ton of cool drinks and snacks, and his parents were hardly ever home. It was without a doubt the best place to watch videos.

Skylar was manning the remote, as he often did, pausing the DVD when skaters popped particularly high ollies or pressing slow motion during a particularly technical trick.

"Cut that out, man, just let the vid play!" JT demanded.

Skylar laughed. "How else are we going to learn tricks? You got to *analyze* to *utilize*, you know what I mean?"

"Slow-mo is lame. It makes the vid lose momentum."

Cale agreed with Skylar but he would never speak up in the presence of JT. Watching tricks in slow motion, Cale would ask himself questions about how the pros did it: Where did they place their feet before tricks? At what angle did they roll up to the obstacle? What part of their board did they slide or grind? Skate videos, in Cale's opinion, were sacred things that held the key to the secrets of skateboarding. Watching them made Cale feel that anything was possible, as if, in some way, he was actually watching himself in the video, performing perfectly.

"We should skate over to Toby's today and get some practice in," said JT, as Cale ejected the video from Skylar's DVD player and slid it carefully back into its shiny blue plastic case.

"Let's do it," said Skylar.

It was the first day of spring break and the nicest day of the year so far. Cale was actually sweating as he ripped through the streets of Drayton with JT, Skylar, and Josh. Watching the video had gotten them pumped. The warm breeze and the smell of spring swirling around excited them even more.

JT skated out in front of the crew and the strong, warm breeze ripped through his longish brown hair. Skylar was right behind him, drafting him for speed and trying to pass him for fun. Cale came third, carving down the hill as they passed the bowling alley and the fish and chip shop. Josh was bringing up the rear. Today the video camera was apparently giving him no problems, and he was acting as follow cam as the crew tore through the streets. To imitate the style of most skate videos, Josh had bought a wide-angle fisheye lens, which was attached to the barrel of his camera now. His camera light would help capture late-night footage.

The SSC had worked out the best route to Toby's, the one that gave the smoothest ride and had the best obstacles on the way. Already, the guys were planning their tricks: the slide or grind they'd do on the electrical box or what they would attempt on the perfect, naturally formed hip in front of the nursery school.

With the camera following them, they felt like they were the stars of their own skate video, and JT let out a loud "whoop!" as Skylar landed a perfect three-sixty flip off a little bump on a sewer grate. Skylar shouted "Yeah!" when Cale spun a little nollie-heelflip. JT scratched a perfect crooked grind on the electrical box and rolled away fakie. Skylar followed up, opting for a frontside boardslide, and landed it, too. Now it was Cale's turn and the pressure was on, since Josh was filming, and so far, the footage had been flawless. He too opted for a boardslide, but different: a near-perfect lipslide across the green metal box. But he made a sketchy landing, his heel dragging a bit on the ground and messing up his next couple of pushes. That annoyed him.

When JT landed a huge backside ollie over the hip as they passed the nursery school, Cale's cheer of encouragement came out more like a squeak from a dying mouse. Cale just looked at the ground and hoped that the growl of their skate wheels had obscured any whimper he'd let out.

When they rounded the corner into King's Court, they were amazed to see a flurry of activity. Not skating but rather a bunch of older skaters from the neighbourhood helping Toby's dad, Russ, make improvements to the ramps and obstacles on the street. A few of Russ's friends were also there, who were all in their thirties.

As they rolled closer, Cale could see Mark Skinner with a pencil between his teeth and an electric jigsaw in his hand. Mark was taller than everybody and his tanned skin always made it look like he'd just come back from a vacation. His crisp black baseball cap was turned a bit sideways on his head, covering his short, dark brown hair. Mark nodded in the direction of the crew as they rolled up. Russ was beside Mark, checking out some plans on a piece of paper. Cale figured they were building some kind of pyramid or funbox, with a handrail on one side and a low hubba on the other. Toby came out from the garage and smiled when he saw Cale and the Seven Stair Crew.

"Oh, look — it's the biggest poser in Drayton," JT said, just loud enough for only Cale and the Seven Stair Crew to hear.

"Hey, dudes!" Toby said, nearly tripping over the two-by-four he was dragging along. Toby was small, a little chubby, and always seemed to be wearing clothes that were two sizes too big. He had a strange way of talking that made it sound as if he was slightly out of breath and there was way too much saliva in his mouth.

"What are you building, Pose-y? I mean, Toby?" asked JT, pretending he didn't really care.

"A ten-foot-long platform, two slant ramps, a hip and a couple of rails, and two *really* big quarterpipes," Toby blurted out proudly. He must have missed the fact that JT insulted him, or he was so used to it he pretended it didn't bother him.

"This is all going to be finished for Saturday?" Skylar asked, raising his eyebrows.

"If everything goes right, it should be finished by end of day tomorrow," Russ said.

"Hey, if you guys help out, maybe it'd even be done sooner."

For the next hour or so, everybody worked together in near silence, except for the occasional grunting or Russ asking Toby to go inside and grab a big jug of lemonade for the workers. Cale and Skylar got loads of wood from the garage, and JT and Josh swung hammers and knocked the splintery sheets of plywood into place. When Russ was satisfied that they'd done enough for the day, the newest obstacle had fully taken shape and it looked so awesome.

"All we have to do is add the Masonite and she's done," Russ announced.

Cale had been paying attention to his work and hadn't really noticed what else had been going on around the street. So when he looked across the road and saw Sarah Leahman and Angie Dunlop doing cartwheels and goofing around on Sarah's lawn, he was a caught off guard. He knew the girls from school — Sarah was in his class and Angie was in the same grade but had a different teacher. He would never admit it, but something about Angie had always fascinated him. She had long dark hair and deep brown eyes. She didn't talk a lot, but when she did, her raspy voice made him melt. Of course, he would never admit this to his friends. He knew Angie was a great basketball player, too. He once peeked into the small windows in the school gym and saw her shooting hoops at team practice. It seemed like she never missed.

Cale liked Sarah, too, but in a different way, more as a friend. But Angie — something about her made him feel nervous and excited at the same time. Now there they were, two girls, giggling and practising gymnastics on the lawn across the road. Even though he knew them both, no way would he ever go and talk to them. Then Angie, laughing about something with Sarah, did a somersault, and as she finished, her eyes met Cale's. He had to do something, so he casually smiled, raised his hand, and gave her a small wave, acting as cool as he knew how. Incredibly, Angie smiled a bright, beautiful smile and waved back.

The moment was broken when Toby bumped into Cale while grabbing a skateboard that was lying on the grass nearby. "Can we skate it now, Dad?" Toby asked, rolling toward one of the slant ramps and kicking a turn halfway up it.

"Not unless you want to get a handful of slivers in your butt, buddy. We'll have to wait till we get the Masonite on 'er," Russ said, wiping his brow with his striped sweatband.

The work crew, even the older guys who didn't skate, headed for the backyard where a mini-ramp session was about to get underway. Cale didn't feel like riding the mini-ramp and sharing a sweaty helmet with one of the older guys.

"I think we should go skate somewhere else," Cale said to JT.

"Where do you wanna go?" JT asked.

"Maybe over to the school or just skate some flat ground behind the grocery store. I dunno," Cale said.

Just then, Mark, who had been helping put away the power tools, came down the driveway toward the crew.

"Hey, listen, we're gonna take D-Mac's pickup downtown tonight. We normally leave about nine and come back to Drayton at, like, midnight. So anyway, if you wanna come, just meet us at the shop at like ten to nine tonight." Mark turned on his heels and walked to pick up his skateboard, which was lying on the lawn.

Cale's jaw dropped. Here was Mark, the coolest guy and the best skater in town, asking if the Seven Stair Crew (plus Cale) wanted to skate in the big city. It was almost too much to believe.

"There's no way my parents would ever let me go," Skylar said.

"You can count me out, too," Josh echoed.

JT looked at Cale.

"You think your mom would let you go, man?" he asked.

Cale thought it over for a second. "Maybe," he shrugged.

As they rolled away from Toby's place, Cale started to plan. He'd never really lied to his mom before, well, at least not a big lie. But he really wanted to go to the big city and skate with Mark, and he was almost sure that his mom wouldn't let him.

Cale wondered if he could arrange to sleep over at JT's house. Then they could both go, and Mom would never know. *What's the worst that could happen?* he asked himself. After all, he'd be going to sleep around 12:30 a.m., and he'd stayed up that late before during school holidays.

On the way back home, Cale and JT stopped at George's Convenience to grab a drink and some snacks. Cale had never spent even this much time alone with JT, let alone sleep over. They were sitting on their decks, the last rays of the March sun casting a pinkish light on the world, when Cale got up the courage to break the silence.

"JT, are your parents going to be cool with you going downtown with Mark and those guys?" Cale asked, popping a few chips into his mouth. His palms were sweating.

"Whatever. My mom won't care," he said.

"Do you think I could sleep at your place?" Cale asked.

"Whattaya mean? Why do you want to sleep over at my place?"

"Well, I'll tell my mom that we're going to have a sleepover at your place and, uh, then I can go skating downtown with you and the guys," Cale explained, thinking that there was no way JT would say yes.

JT thought about it for a good ten seconds before he replied. "Alright, but you're gonna have to sleep on my floor, and, uh, you can't tell the other guys about where I live."

Cale was so elated that JT had agreed, it took him a few seconds to register the second part of what JT said.

"Uh, yeah, I'm cool to sleep on the floor and I won't say anything, or whatever," Cale assured him, not quite clear what he was agreeing to.

Cale wiped off his hands and threw his chip bag into the yellow trash can in front of George's. "Alright, here goes nothing," Cale said, and the two of them skated toward Cale's place.

When they arrived, they placed their boards against the side of the house and went inside. Cale's mom was whistling to herself in the kitchen. Cale and JT took their shoes off and hopped up the small flight of stairs that led to the kitchen.

"Um, can I sleep over at JT's? It's fine with his parents and everything. I'll go to bed at my normal bedtime and everything. Can I?" Cale said without taking a breath.

Cale's mom wiped her hands on her apron and eyed Cale with slight suspicion. "Are you sure your parents have no problem with Cale staying the night?" she asked JT.

"No, they'll be cool, it's just my mom and her boyfriend Ken, and they said they were fine with it," JT said.

"Would it be alright if I gave your mom a quick call right now to check?"

"Sure," said JT. "Oh, wait, you know what, actually, she said she was going to go shopping to get us something for dinner. I just remembered."

Cale was amazed at how quick-thinking JT was.

"Well, isn't that nice of her," Cale's mom said to JT before turning to Cale. "Don't forget to pack your toothbrush, honey."

Cale bolted up the stairs. *The quicker I get out of here, the better*, he thought.

He ran into his room and threw a pair of jeans, two T-shirts, and his hooded sweatshirt into his backpack. When he came back downstairs, he couldn't see his mom or JT.

"Mom!" he called out.

"Down here, Cale," she shouted up from her studio.

Cale slunk down the basement stairs and heard JT and his mom talking. She was showing him her newest painting, of an old warplane sitting at the bottom of the ocean.

"It's a DC-3, isn't it?" JT asked. "Actually, with a camo paint job like that, I guess it's a C-47. Either way, it looks like it's down there for good."

Cale's mom smiled. "Wow, you know your planes. It is a C-47. It's in an airplane graveyard just off the coast of Florida. I'm painting it for the warplane museum."

"How did you learn to paint like that, Mrs. Finch?" JT asked.

"Oh, call me Margot," she said. "Well, first, I've always loved to draw and paint, and I also did four years of art school. But it's like anything, practice makes perfect. How do you know so much about old planes?"

"I've always really loved reading books about history, war history especially," JT said.

"You ready to go?" asked Cale from the stairs. He was afraid to linger a minute more than necessary.

"Wait just one second, young man!" Cale's mom said.

Cale stiffened.

"You're not going anywhere without giving your mom a hug," she insisted.

"Mo-om!" Cale said with embarrassment. He trudged toward her, pretending that having to hug his mom was some kind of punishment.

"You be good, young man. I have JT's home number, and you never know, I may call to check up on you." She gave him a big hug and Cale pushed aside a small twinge of guilt.

JT and Cale bounded back up the stairs, grabbed their boards from the side of the house, and headed out into the night. As they rolled away from the house, Cale began to feel a sense of freedom he'd never experienced before. He felt as though the night held a brand-new world of boundless possibilities. He also felt a pang of worry in his belly. His mom had been kidding about calling, but only sort of. Cale knew there was a possibility that she might actually call, and he didn't know what would happen if she discovered he wasn't at JT's after all.

CHAPTER 4
INTO THE CITY

JT and Cale heard the music from the pickup truck when it pulled into the parking lot behind Drayton Skates. It was 9:05 p.m., and they'd been waiting for the older guys for more than fifteen minutes without saying a word to each another. They would have waited all night if it came to that. Cale picked up his backpack and JT pulled the hood of his sweatshirt over his long hair as they walked slowly around to the back of the shop. Cale felt like sprinting, but thought it was better to act casual in the presence of these older guys. He was nervous and didn't want to mess anything up.

When they came around the corner, they saw a guy in the driver's seat of the little black Mazda pickup and two other guys in the back. Mark was nowhere to be seen.

JT recognized one of the guys in the back.

"Hey, Greg! he said, lifting his board in the air as a greeting.

"Yo, it's the grommets!" said the driver, before Greg could respond.

Being called a grommet was a bit of an insult, but Cale knew it was also a half-hearted sign of acceptance, so he and JT hopped up on the back bumper of the truck and flung themselves in the bucket without saying a word. JT bumped fists with Greg as Greg introduced the other guy in the back as Chavo. Chavo did nothing but nod, turn his headphones up a little louder, and wiggle his butt to try and get more comfortable on the metal floor.

"Where's Mark?" asked Cale.

"Oh, he's inside grabbin' some stuff," said Greg.

The rear door of the shop swung open and Mark jumped out carrying a box jammed with stuff and a camera bag. He slammed the huge metal door behind him, set the box down, and then slid his key into the lock, pulling on the door to make sure it was shut properly.

"Hey, dudes!" Mark called out over his shoulder. "Got somethin' for ya, Cale."

Cale felt singled out until Mark threw the camera bag and box into the front seat and came around the back giving high-fives to everybody. From behind his back, Mark pulled out a shoebox and handed it to Cale. His new shoes!

"And here's your change," Mark said, jamming a scrunched-up five-dollar bill into Cale's palm.

Until this point, Cale had felt like they were tagging along with a bunch of dudes who didn't really want them there. Now, with Mark handing Cale the new kicks, he felt like he was really part of the group.

"You sure it's cool with your parents for you guys to come?" Mark asked, lifting an eyebrow of doubt.

Cale nodded as he set to work sliding the laces into his new shoes.

"Cool," said Mark. "My parents sure wouldn't have let me come when I was your age. Anyway, when we get on the highway, you guys better keep your heads down, alright?"

Mark hopped into the front seat and stuck his head out as the driver threw the truck into reverse and cranked the volume on the stereo.

"And one more thing," Mark yelled over the racket, "hold on!"

The pickup squealed out of the parking lot, onto the main street, and turned right, toward the highway. The engine of the truck made a low grumble, but it seemed to be driving fine, so Cale guessed the sound was sort of normal. They went down a big hill that made Cale's stomach rise into his throat. Cale smiled at JT, who just smirked back a bit. He didn't want to act too excited in front of these older guys, but it was really hard to hold it in on a night like this. The truck swerved onto the on-ramp of the highway and the driver gunned the engine. Cale watched the night world whiz by at what seemed like a million miles an hour.

He could see the glow of lights from the big city, rising into the night with a magnetic radiance that seemed to pull the truck closer and closer. Cale imagined that it was some distant kingdom and that he and the others in the truck were some kind of modern-day knights about to vanquish it. Cale knew that out of the group, Mark would have been the king, and everyone else his subjects. *Mark is a true street king,* Cale thought. The wind got a bit cooler and Cale popped his head back down behind the truck's cab, tucking his hands into his armpits and pulling his hood up. He then laid himself down and listened to the noise of the wheels on the road, vibrating up through the truck box. It was a strange sound but somehow comforting. His face was out of the wind, and all he could hear was his breath and his heartbeat as the truck sped further and further away from Drayton.

When they pulled into the core of the city, it was almost ten p.m. The truck zoomed toward the banking district — the best place to skate. The slabs of marble and smooth stairs outside the bank towers seemed almost made for skating, especially at night. Cale craned his head around and could see that the banking district was deserted, except for the odd security guard inside the foyers of the buildings or the homeless guys sleeping in the warm air that blew upwards from the grates outside.

The driver, D-Mac, rolled the truck to a stop on a side street. He got out of the front seat and stretched his arms into the air, groaning a bit. He came around to the side of the truck and looked at Cale, then JT.

"I'm gonna need some gas money from you guys for the way home 'kay?" he said nonchalantly.

JT shot Cale a worried glance. Cale tried to stay cool. "No problem, man," he said.

D-Mac grabbed a skateboard and the video camera bag from the front seat and everyone began piling out of the back of the truck.

"Guess this is where we're parking," said Greg, ollieing up a curb and attempting a manual on the sidewalk.

Mark opened the box in the front seat and inside were three brand-new decks, all without graphics or a lick of paint.

"Where'd you get those?" Cale asked, as Mark expertly laid grip tape on the top of the board and smoothed it out with a loose skateboard wheel.

"Darius at Drayton Skates gives 'em to me," he said. "Guess it's one of the perks of being shop-sponsored. Hey, how are those new shoes?"

"Great!" Cale said, thinking about how awesome it would be to get a sponsor and have free boards whenever he wanted. Although his board was in good shape, it was his first one in almost a year. His old one was a Dave Henson pro model and he had skated it down to a sliver. Both the nose and tail were so chipped up there was almost nothing left of them. Cale's new board was a REWL team deck — which meant it wasn't a pro model and that made it about four bucks cheaper. The graphics on it were plain maroon and blue stripes that went horizontally across the bottom. Cale had added a few strategically placed stickers to jazz it up a bit.

Cale leaned into the bed of the pickup and grabbed his old shoes. Rolling toward a large marble trash can, Cale was stopped short by JT. "What are you doing, man?" JT asked.

"Just trashin' my old shoes."

"I'll take 'em," JT said, reaching out his hand.

Cale looked down at JT's shoes and saw that they were actually in rougher shape than the ones he was about to toss. He looked down at his new shoes and felt a pang of guilt at their newness, before he remembered how much work he'd done to save for them.

"Sure, have 'em," Cale said, proud to think that JT would actually be wearing his old stuff.

Mark was almost finished putting the trucks on his new set-up, twisting the final bolt in with an Allen key. Everybody had been trying a few tricks around the truck, but they were all silently waiting for Mark.

"Alright," Mark said, standing on his board, flexing his ankles to test the trucks. "Let's do this."

Cale threw his small backpack into the cab of the truck just as D-Mac locked the door with his key. D-Mac shot Cale a disparaging glance as if to say, "Why are you here?" then slung the camera bag over his shoulder and called out to whomever would listen.

"Listen up, dudes, this truck leaves at twelve-thirty a.m. If you're not here, it leaves without you." He narrowed his eyes, singling out JT and Cale. "Especially *you,* grommets," he said. "You get split up from the group, you gotta find your own way home."

Mark rolled by Cale and JT. "Don't worry about him," Mark said. "His girlfriend just dumped him."

Cale snickered a bit under his breath and then watched as Mark ollied swiftly up a curb and rolled down the smooth sidewalk. Everybody followed, like a pack of dogs.

Cale lifted his head and looked at the huge buildings that reached like modern castle spires way up into the night sky. Most of the lights were on in the skyscrapers and the light cast an eerie glow that made Cale feel like a trespasser in a secret world he did not know.

Mark whistled a high note and beckoned everybody to follow him as he picked up his skateboard by the nose and ran up a flight of five slick black steps. Cale read the sign, Trader's Insurance Building, adding to his mental list of landmarks that might steer him back to the truck if he got separated from the group.

Cale flicked his board into his hand and climbed the stairs behind the group. He was closing in and could see Mark way up ahead, setting up for a trick. Mark ollied up onto a ledge, and with his speed carrying him, rolled along the ledge to a drop-off. Mark effortlessly nollied a perfect kickflip into the night and Cale heard the unmistakable sound of a perfect landing.

Next up, Chavo ollied up onto the ledge, messed up his footing, and stepped off his board. But he grabbed his front truck and got out of the way in time for the next skater. It was JT; somehow, he'd positioned himself third. He ignored the ledge and drop altogether, opting instead for the stairs beside them. He snapped a big hardflip, backlit by the soft glow from the lights of the buildings.

Greg was next and he scratched a frontside one-eighty ollie down the five steps. He landed it, but from Cale's vantage point, the landing lacked style and looked lame.

D-Mac rolled toward the stairs and slid his foot to stop. As Cale was approaching, D-Mac lifted the viewfinder of the camera, switched on a bright light, and began filming Cale as he rolled toward the stairs. Cale had been running a list of tricks through his mind. At first, he thought he might float a heelflip down the stairs, but since the bright light from the camera hindered his view of the landing, he decided not to try a flip-trick as his first move. The ledge that Mark had no problem ollieing up on was really high — almost up to Cale's knees. Before he could think any more about it, Cale had ollied up onto the ledge and was beginning a perfectly smooth nose-manual across the black marble of the ledge. He surprised even himself, teetering on just the front two wheels of his board. As he approached the edge of the ledge, he pushed down hard with his front foot and levelled his tail out with his back foot. The light from the camera shone down and spotted his landing for him, and a little voice in his head called out, "You're actually going to land this!" Which he did.

A chorus of "yeahs" echoed in the canyon of the buildings, and a shudder of exhilaration shot into Cale's hands. The manual wasn't long, maybe eight feet at most, but he had come off clean and earned the respect of the older guys.

"Nice," said Greg, flipping his hand up and throwing Cale a high-five.

Cale played it cool and rolled to JT.

"I saw your hardflip, man. It was sweet," Cale said.

JT just gave a big smile and bumped fists with Cale.

The light of the video camera switched off and Mark was already skating away with speed. D-Mac put the camera away and followed. The night was just beginning.

Mark was skating so fast through the streets that no one could catch him. Everyone was at least thirty feet behind him as he wove through the sparse traffic and ollied up a curb, heading toward the huge front entrance of a brightly lit bank building. When Cale got closer and the spot they were about to hit came into view, he swallowed a gulp of air and a blast of adrenaline shot through his entire body. The building in front of him was a skater's paradise!

Golden handrails cascaded from the pink marble at every conceivable angle. Huge slabs of marble that were benches during the day were perfect for long grinds and smooth manuals. Stairs grew in clusters of three, five, and a double set of six with a five-foot landing between them.

Mark skidded to a stop, just shy of where the huge lights lit the atrium. "We've got about ten minutes of skating before we get busted by security." Turning, Mark continued. "D-Mac, I really want to get a three-sixty flip down the double set. And if I get that, I want to try a nose-grind or something on one of the rails."

D-Mac just nodded and rolled toward the bottom of the double set. Nobody moved.

"Well?" Mark said as he looked at the gang with a smile on his face. "What are you waiting for?"

It was on. Cale went immediately over to one of the huge marble slabs and proceeded to crooked-grind the whole thing. The skaters set about the front of the bank like a horde of marauders, spreading out and ripping up the benches, ollieing the stairs, and sliding the rails. Cale rolled around the plaza a bit and took a look at one of the perfect square golden handrails that was angled over a set of four pink marble stairs. He had never slid a "real" handrail before, just handrails in skate parks, which tended to be lower and not overtop stairs. He had it in his mind that tonight he was going to slide his first real handrail.

Then, everyone stopped their skating and looked up at Mark, who had climbed to the top of the double set to the right of the group. Holding his board by the nose he ran a few steps for speed, jumped on his board, and tore toward the top step. The distance he would have to clear was massive, so he pushed four big pushes in quick succession. With D-Mac filming, Mark bent low and snapped a controlled three-sixty flip under his feet. As he floated over the double set, for some reason the board arched an extra flip, and Mark landed on the board while it was upside-down. His new deck scraped to a halt at the bottom of the stairs.

He slid onto his back and did a reverse somersault in a perfect aversion to a bad bail. He shook his head, grabbed his board, and bounded up the stairs again for a second try.

Gone was the super-friendly, easygoing Mark. Now his eyes were like little black coals and his mouth a slash of concentration. He popped his tail and the board began a slower but higher arc than before. He caught it on his feet perfectly as the second set of stairs began, and navigated it to the ground. But then the board stopped dead in its tracks and Mark landed on his chest with a thud before rolling away onto his back.

"Oh, dude!" D-Mac said, setting the camera down and rushing to his side.

Mark didn't say anything, and with a little wave just sent D-Mac away. Mark took a few deep breaths, groaned, and then rose to his feet and dusted his hands off on his jeans.

Cale wondered if Mark would try it again. In the meantime, he decided to give the handrail a try. He called JT over.

"Hey, JT, check out this handrail!"

JT rolled toward Cale, popping a perfect nollie heel in the process. Cale knew that JT had slid real handrails in the past. In Drayton, there were really only two good handrails. One was at the bank, and every time a skater tried to skate it, they'd get kicked out by the bank manager. The other handrail was at the nursery school. It was short, painted brown, and not all that fun to skate. JT, who rode regular, could do backside boardslides on it at the drop of a hat, but Cale had a hard time with the run-up and the landing. The landing was either dusty grass or mud, depending on the season. JT took a look at the handrail that Cale was about to slide.

"Be careful," JT said. "That's a big ollie."

Cale knew JT was right. He would have to ollie really high just to get his board in a position to land on the rail and centre himself. He'd have to come at the thing on an angle, too, which added to the complexity.

Cale took two big pushes and rolled toward the shimmering handrail. He swung a swift turn around the marble bench and headed dead at the rail, which now looked even taller than it had before. Just before he bent his knees in preparation, a deep booming voice echoed in the atrium.

"Get outta here!"

CHAPTER 5
SHATTERED

Cale stepped off his board and whipped his head around to source out the threatening voice. Two security guards were coming out of a revolving door at the west end of the building, one younger and one a bald old guy with a moustache. Chavo and Greg didn't stop skating, even though the guards were now pointing at Chavo with their walkie-talkies.

Cale couldn't believe how relaxed Chavo was acting. Here were two huge guys not ten feet away and Chavo was still trying to land a fifty-fifty grind to bigspin.

Cale looked up to the top of the double set, where Mark stood, checking out the situation. He had been right; they'd been skating about ten minutes and now the fun was over — or was it?

Mark gave a nod to D-Mac, who rolled the camera.

Cale turned back toward the guards, who had Chavo by the scruff of his neck. When they pulled off his hood, it became obvious why Chavo had been ignoring them. His headphones were on and his music must have been cranked. The bald security guard pulled out one of the white ear buds and yelled at Chavo point blank.

"Leave, now! Before we call the police!"

Chavo looked stunned. He scurried toward his board, picked it up, and rolled away from the lights of the bank's entrance.

Cale heard Mark's wheels hit the ground at the top of the double set and turned back toward him. Mark was under the most pressure, on this, his third attempt. He had already slammed twice, and he had security walking toward him. Make that jogging toward him. Cale had to step out of the way of the two giant enforcers as they ran toward Mark and D-Mac.

"Hey!" one of them yelled.

"Hey you, stop!" screamed the other.

But they were too late. Mark was already in the midst of a perfectly popped three-flip. He caught it on his feet and drifted down the remainder of the impossibly long double set. He landed the trick perfectly and rode away with speed, giving the two security guards a wave as he disappeared into the night. The rest of the skaters, including Cale, followed Mark, and like a pack of wolves, they all began to howl. It was the thrill of the amazingly landed trick and a clean getaway that made their adrenaline surge and their voices call out in manic yelps.

"I can't believe that!" D-Mac said, patting Mark on the back as they rolled to the next spot. "I'm pretty sure I got the whole thing, too!"

Mark was smiling as the breeze flicked at his T-shirt. The rest of the guys bringing up the rear were laughing and talking about Chavo's run-in with the security guards.

Mark hopped up a curb and continued his role of tour guide as the guys raced further south toward the Central Station banks, which were two sets of concrete slabs sloped in front of the city's enormous train station. The banks were lit by two huge spotlights that shone up to a large piece of art, a massive steel, oval-shaped cage with a giant locomotive inside, as if the engine itself were the centre of some atom of progress. It made the skate spot kind of intimidating and made Cale feel even smaller than his five-foot-one frame. But it made an amazing background for still shots and video footage.

D-Mac skated up to Cale as Greg and JT began to roll around on the steep banks, popping little shifties and frontside ollies. Mark and Chavo skated off by themselves into the darkness.

"Watch my stuff, grommet," D-Mac ordered Cale, and he skated off to catch up to Mark and Chavo.

Cale didn't have a choice. He simply sat on his skateboard and leaned against D-Mac's big over-the-shoulder camera bag.

"Where do you think they're going?" Cale asked JT, who was now trying frontside blunt slides on a little curb at the bottom of the banks.

"Beats me," JT said. Then he nonchalantly added, "Hey, do you think your mom would actually call my house?"

A pang of worry rose up in Cale. He'd been so wrapped up in the excitement of the night it hadn't crossed his mind.

"Oh, man," Cale said. "I totally forgot about that."

JT continued to roll around the front of the station. "Don't worry," he said. "I gave her the wrong number anyway."

"So what number did you give her instead?" Cale pressed, relieved but curious.

JT popped a little nollie and replied, "I gave her my home number, but one of the nines, I drew sort of like a four. So if she asks us why the number didn't work, I'll just tell her that's how I write my nines."

Cale thought it was brilliant and absolutely foolproof. Again, he was amazed at how easily this sort of thing came to JT. At the same time, he felt awful that he and JT were tricking his mom.

A few minutes later, Mark came ripping out of the darkness with a big goofy grin on his face and proceeded to slash a long five-o grind along the top of one of the banks. Cale really wanted to prove himself to Mark, so he popped up from the ground and skated toward the steep banks with the plan of attempting a kickflip to fakie. As he got close, D-Mac called out to him.

"Hey, grom! You're supposed to be watching my stuff, man!" Cale stopped skating and circled back.

"Sorry, man, I just thought —"

"You just thought what? That all I wanted to do tonight was film? I wanna skate for once, too!"

With that, D-Mac rolled to the bank and gave Chavo a high-five. Cale felt bruised on his insides, like he'd done something wrong, even though he knew he hadn't. He wanted to tell Mark that D-Mac was being a jerk, but what would that get him? He figured he just had to suck it up as he wasn't the kind of kid to smart mouth older guys anyway. So he sat with the camera gear and took a break from skating.

Mark tried to ollie the gap between the two banks, came close a couple of times, but then rolled his ankle and came over to sit beside Cale.

"Why aren't you skating?" Mark asked.

"I'm watching this stuff for D-Mac," Cale said matter-of-factly. D-Mac was nowhere in sight.

"I'll watch the gear for a while if you want to skate," Mark offered.

Cale didn't even give it a second thought. He hopped on his board and rolled away.

Cale had the perfect amount of speed as he rolled up the steep incline of the bank and flipped a perfect backside kickflip as he reached the top. Mid-air, Cale felt like he was in slow motion, floating above the city. He caught the board on his feet and absorbed the bank as he touched down. The sensation was electric.

"Yeah!" Mark yelled as Cale rolled back toward him, the feeling of the landing still buzzing through him. Cale smiled at Mark and then rolled around the statue beside the main doors to see what the older guys were up to. D-Mac, Greg, and Chavo were behind the statue, laughing hysterically as they tried to ollie a bright yellow fire hydrant. He wondered if any of them had seen his trick. He rounded the corner just as D-Mac was approaching the hydrant for another try. Caught off guard by Cale, D–Mac messed up his ollie and his board went shooting out from under him and toward the plate glass of the antique doors of the station. The board had so much speed that it shattered the window and shards of glass rained down on the concrete.

D–Mac was sitting on his butt watching the whole thing happen. Then he turned to Calc.

"You're supposed to be watching the camera, kid! What the hell!"

Before Cale could explain, a loud alarm began to squeal inside the station.

D–Mac ran toward the door, picked up his glass-covered skateboard, and took off with Chavo and Greg. JT rounded the corner behind the statue to check out the commotion and saw Cale standing there, frozen, unsure what to do. He yelled, "Let's get outta here!" and the two of them skated off into the night, trying to follow the others.

When they got to the street, there was no sign of D–Mac, Greg, Chavo, or Mark. They had disappeared. The camera gear was gone, too.

The alarm was still screeching — it was the perfect sound to accompany what was happening inside Cale's body. He was beyond worried. Cale could tell by the look on JT's face that he was nervous, too, but it made them skate faster, away from the scene and into the darkness of an underground parking garage nearby. They stopped just under the fringe of shadow inside the mouth of the garage and waited, out of breath.

Two police cars pulled right up onto the sidewalk of Central Station, their lights flashing.

From where they were hidden, Cale and JT watched as two cops got out of each cruiser and began walking toward the shattered glass of the main doors. Inside, someone — it looked like a maintenance guy — began to undo the heavy brass locks. One of the cops grabbed a walkie-talkie and began speaking into it. He turned around and began to check up and down the street for any clue as to who may have broken the glass.

Cale and JT ducked further out of sight, their hearts racing and their eyes wild with fear. Cale's first instinct was to go and talk to the cops, maybe try to explain their situation. Surely a cop would understand. Before he could suggest his idea to JT, JT had formulated another plan.

"Okay, here's what we do," JT said. "We get to the top of this parking garage, where we've got a view of this part of the city, and we try to see which way the guys have headed."

Without a second thought, Cale and JT began scrambling up the six storeys of concrete stairs to the rooftop. They bolted from the door and began looking over the sides of the massive parking structure to try to spot the older guys. A thought burst into Cale's head and he said it out loud.

"JT, for sure they went back to the truck!"

JT thought about this for a second.

"Do you think you'd be able to get us back there?" JT asked.

Cale thought for a few seconds, then shook his head. "I was watching for landmarks right up until we got busted by those security guards. After that, I stopped thinking about it."

They circled the top of the parking garage a few more times, looking down at the surface streets and hoping to spot the gang in flight.

"There," Cale said, pointing north between two towering buildings.

Way below them was the black Mazda, right where D-Mac had parked it. The truck was just sitting there. It looked like a little toy.

"We've got to get there before they do!" JT said, hopping on his skateboard.

There were two long winding ramps that led from the top floor of the parking garage to street level. One spilled out cars onto National Avenue, right across from Central Station; the other delivered traffic onto a back street. Cale knew they had no time to lose — but which ramp should they take?

JT was already skating toward the nearest one. "Wait, we have to think about this!" said Cale.

"Are you crazy? We just gotta get down there, back to the truck," JT said, shuddering a little.

"No, listen, if we take the wrong one, we might end up back out onto the street in front of the train station. They'd see us for sure! Listen, maybe the cops can help us!" Cale was pleading with JT.

Just then, he noticed a cop car, lights completely off, crawling like a crouching panther up the ramp over JT's shoulder. Cale was unable to speak, but JT could tell by the look in his eyes that something was behind him.

"Go!" JT shouted, and he began running with his board. Cale couldn't make up his mind. Should he go with JT? Try to talk to the cops? After all, he was just a lost kid, and he didn't break the window. The cop car zoomed closer.

"C'mon man!" JT yelled before he was swallowed in the darkness of the ramp. "Hurry!"

Instinct took over. Cale spun quickly and jumped on his board, pushing with all his might and picking up an incredible amount of speed as he headed down the twisting asphalt corkscrew of the other ramp.

The cop car couldn't keep up with JT and Cale as they whipped around corners, barely staying aboard. They could hear the squealing rubber of the cruiser's wheels as it attempted to keep up.

When they got to the bottom, Cale could just make out a yellow chain that went across the parking lot entrance between two yellow metal posts.

"Ollie the chain, JT!" Cale yelled, just in case JT hadn't seen it; but he obviously had, because he snapped a perfectly smooth ollie over the chain and sped out safely onto the street in front of Cale.

Cale bent his knees preparing to ollie the chain, which appeared much higher as he got closer. Doubt flashed through Cale's mind as he went to smack the tail of his board. He was able to eke out an ollie, but it was too low. Way too low. His back truck hung up on the chain and flung him like a rag doll onto the asphalt. He turned back and saw his skateboard swinging on the chain like some bizarre playground equipment. Everything was still.

In the next instant, the lights of the cruiser snapped toward Cale as it rounded the final corner, gunning the accelerator. Cale ran to the mouth of the garage, grabbed the tail of his deck, yanked it from the chain, and turned quickly away from the garage. He jumped on his board and pushed into the darkness in the direction that JT had fled.

The next sound he heard would stay with him forever. It was the squealing of the cop car's tires followed by a loud gut-wrenching smash, and then, the blaring of the cop car's horn for at least five seconds. It was as if the car was mad that it hadn't caught the kid on the skateboard.

Cale finally caught up with JT, and now they were ripping through the streets in the direction of D-Mac's parked truck, hoping, praying that their only way back to Drayton hadn't left. Except for the smooth low grinding of their urethane wheels on the dark pavement, there was not a sound out of either of them. They knew that time was wasting and that there was a chance the other cop car could be looming in the shadows they passed.

With only a few more blocks to go, the un-thinkable happened.

Cale and JT saw the Mazda zipping through a light a couple of streets up. It was too far away to catch. The two boys stopped and JT stuck his thumb and index finger in his mouth to fire out a loud whistle-blast that echoed against the skyscrap-er walls. As the echo drowned under the hum of the city, Cale and JT's hopelessness grew. Then, without warning, a pair of headlights and the squeal of tires came up from behind them.

They turned and froze in the bright lights.

CHAPTER 6
JT'S PLACE

"Get in!" a voice commanded. It was Mark's.

Without a second thought, JT and Cale flung themselves into the rear of the truck, ducked down, and peered over the edge of the box. Everybody in the back was silent. Cale wanted to tell all of the older guys their story, but he would have to wait. Right now, they would be lucky if they got out of the city without getting stopped by the cops.

The little window from the cab opened up and Mark peered into the back. "We thought we'd lost you guys," he said, smiling. "Just keep your heads down."

Halfway home, the truck veered off the highway and pulled into a brightly lit gas station.

D-Mac jumped from the cab and came around the side. "You guys got that gas money?" he asked, looking directly at Cale.

Mark slipped out from the passenger side.

"Relax, D-Mac!" he yawned. "Here!" He flung a twenty-dollar bill onto the hood of the truck and D-Mac snatched it before it blew away.

"What's up with you and those kids, man?" D-Mac said, as he grabbed the nozzle of the gas pump.

"What do you care? Oh, let me guess, you weren't a kid once?" Mark shot back.

As D-Mac muttered something, fumbling with the gas cap, Mark said something that completely floored Cale. "They're both better skaters than you, anyway."

Although he said it under his breath, Cale was pretty sure that everybody, including D-Mac, had gotten the gist of what Mark had said. But D-Mac just stood there, staring at the little digital readout on the gas pump.

Mark then turned to the guys in the back of the truck, signalled toward the gas station's little convenience store and said, "C'mon guys, let's get a Coke or something."

All the guys jumped out from the back and stretched. The air was colder the closer they moved toward Drayton and Cale was glad he'd worn his hooded sweatshirt. He pulled up his hood as they walked into the convenience store.

"So what happened to you guys after we got

separated?" Mark asked, opening the door for JT and Cale.

"We got chased by the cops. Whatever." JT shrugged, like it was no big deal.

In Cale's mind, it was the craziest thing that had ever happened to him. His hands were still shaking and he couldn't get the sound of the cruiser's squealing tires out of his head. He asked Mark, "What happened to you guys?"

"We just split as fast as we could. We lost Chavo for a bit, but when we got to the truck, he was there. I'm glad we saw you when we were takin' off," he said.

Cale grabbed a small bag of peanuts and a lemonade.

"Mark, did you tell D-Mac that you said you'd watch the camera?" Cale asked.

"Something like that," Mark replied. "Don't worry, D-Mac knows it wasn't your fault the window got broke."

JT grabbed a Coke and a bag of chips sheepishly and walked up to Cale.

"Hey, Cale, do you think you could lend me the money to get these?" he asked.

"Sure, man," Cale said, pulling out the rumpled five-dollar bill Mark had given him at the start of the night.

Cale yawned, his jaw shaking. "What time is it?" he asked to whomever was listening.

"Almost one," said Mark, walking back to the truck and throwing a can of iced tea to D-Mac, who caught it without even looking.

When the truck hit the highway again, Cale began to recognize a few of the landmarks around Drayton, and knew they would be home soon. Cale always used landmarks and made little maps in his mind to understand his surroundings better. He often drew maps of particular skate spots or schools, picturing himself standing or skating there from above. Cale carried a map of the Seven Stairs plaza in the pocket of his backpack at all times. It had taken him three attempts to draw it perfectly, but now he had a version he thought was pretty accurate. He never told the guys about the map, figuring they'd think it was a dorky thing to draw. But the map gave him ideas about what tricks to try and where to try them. His most ambitious project (still a work in progress) was a map of the whole town of Drayton. It was a great way to waste time in class waiting for the bell to ring.

As the truck drew closer to Drayton, a hazy vision began to form in Cale's exhausted mind. It was a bird's-eye view of King's Court, with all the ramps and obstacles laid out. In a dreamlike way, Cale began to picture himself skating every-thing effortlessly. Then the truck hit a bump and snapped him out of his trance, but not before he had formulated a plan: he would draw a map of Toby's street, just as he'd envisioned it. Then, he would study the map and plan a perfect contest run. Once he'd done that, he'd have the confi-dence to sign up for the contest.

★   ★   ★

D–Mac finally pulled the truck into the back park-ing lot of Drayton Skates, and the guys piled out of the back and began to go their separate ways without much of a goodbye. Cale thought they all looked like zombies, with their eyes puffy and red from no sleep and the cold wind that had been blowing in their faces for the entire ride home.

Mark grabbed his stuff from the front seat of the truck and waved goodbye to Cale and JT. "Later, guys!" Mark called. "Next time I see you, I want the full story of what happened!"

"We will, man," Cale shouted back. But he was so exhausted that even thinking about their insane downtown adventure made him tired. He looked at JT, who was shivering and trying to keep his hands warm by pulling them into the sleeves of his sweatshirt. Around JT's neck, Cale's old skate shoes dangled, laces tied together.

"You still comin' to my place?" JT asked.

"Yeah, if that's okay," Cale replied, thinking that even a floor would be comfortable at this point.

"But remember what you promised, right?" JT said.

"Yeah," Cale said with a shrug.

As they hopped on their boards and stiffly rode into the blackness, Cale wondered how bad it would be at JT's house that he didn't want anyone to know where he lived. Cale had seen some of the run-down houses in Drayton when he'd delivered Christmas meals one year with his mom. They weren't falling down or anything. They had lawns and cars and they weren't that shabby, they just weren't well kept. A few of them had some broken windows and dirt running down the siding, but people lived in them.

JT skated in front of Cale as they headed north through town. They picked up their boards as they crossed over the tracks, and then jumped back on and headed past the fancy houses where Skylar lived and down the big swooping hill that wound itself around the shampoo factory. Cale and JT sliced around the corner, heading toward the shabbier streets up ahead, the part of Drayton that people jokingly referred to as "the wrong side of the tracks." They passed Hoover and approached South Line, their wheels rumbling a little louder over the rougher pavement. There was garbage all over the road from a garbage can that some animal must have gotten into, and Cale had to push tentatively to get around the fast-food drink lids and smooshed packets of ketchup. A plastic bag floated across the road like a silent ghost that had come out to warn them of something.

JT stepped off his skateboard at the end of South Line and began to walk down a little footpath. Cale followed. Lifting a section of chain-link fencing, JT motioned to Cale to duck under it.

"It's better if we go this way," JT whispered.

Part of Cale was intrigued by this detour to wherever it was that JT lived. The other part of him was terrified. He was in a strange part of town, the end of South Line, in the wee hours of the morning. It might as well have been another country.

"Where are we going?" Cale asked, hoping that maybe JT was just playing a practical joke on him and they were about to turn back.

"My mom's," JT replied. "We're almost there."

Around a large unkempt cedar hedge, the moon lit up a stand of tall pine trees and a little silver mobile home tucked up against them. Although the lawn in front of them was strewn with old pieces of plywood and a rusty old riding lawn mower, the place looked kind of inviting. A TV flickered from inside, casting a blue light that matched the moon's glow.

"Be really quiet, dude," JT said. "Or we'll wake her up."

They slunk across the long damp grass, careful not to step on any random bits of refuse the yard had to offer. Cale followed closely behind JT. They set their skateboards down delicately on a red picnic table that was set up nearby on a few cracked patio stones. JT put a finger to his lips and raised his eyebrows at Cale, then pulled the latch on the door. Light spilled out from inside. The TV was buzzing static, and as Cale peered in, he could see a lump under a green blanket, which he assumed was JT's Mom. JT stepped inside and motioned Cale past him down a small, wood-panelled hallway. Halfway down, Cale looked back. JT had turned off the TV and walked over to his mom. He took off her glasses, gave her a kiss on the forehead, and flicked off a small wall-mounted light.

This was the first time Cale had ever seen JT show any kind of affection to anyone, besides the occasional bumping of fists or saying "Hey, what's up?" to his friends. Cale wondered which was the real JT, this one or the one who was so harsh with kids like Toby.

JT squeezed by Cale in the darkness and flicked a light on, illuminating his room. It was just big enough to fit a single bed and a tiny desk. The floor was covered in socks and belts and candy wrappers, with a few ripped-up old skate magazines thrown about.

"You want something to drink? A Pepsi or something?" JT asked quietly.

"No, I'm fine," Cale said, taking off his new shoes and moving aside some of the debris.

"Let me getcha a sleeping bag," JT said, disappearing down the hallway.

Cale looked around the room again. A few skateboard posters and a framed picture of a fighter plane were on the wall, as well as some broken decks that had been screwed right into the panelling. Cale sat on the cold floor and began thumbing through an issue of *Sequence* that was at least fifteen years old. The pictures were of skateboarders in baggy pants doing strange tricks that Cale had never seen, on boards with tiny wheels. He yawned and cleared an even bigger area to be his bed.

JT slid into the small room and closed the tiny

door behind him, tossing a sleeping bag to Cale. Cale wrapped himself up in the coolness of the material, put his head on his shoes and sweatshirt, and fell immediately asleep.

CHAPTER 7
A HARSH WAKE UP

The sound of barking dogs woke Cale. He opened his eyes and looked around the little room. He could see the bright rays of morning sun streaming through the horizontal blinds and illuminating little bits of dust in the air. *Where am I?* he thought for a second, before remembering that he was on JT's floor in a trailer somewhere off the end of South Line. Cale felt stiff, having slept all night on the cold floor, and as he lifted his arms to stretch and let out a big yawn, he noticed that JT wasn't in the low bed beside him.

Cale scratched his head and nervously tiptoed out of the room and into the main room of the trailer. It was empty. Then he heard voices coming from outside. He opened the little door and saw JT and his mom sitting at the small red picnic table. Cale hoped they weren't talking about him.

JT's mom was pretty young and quite thin. She had rough skin and an even rougher voice. She was dressed in the uniform worn by the ladies who poured coffee for old people at the lunch counter in the Zingers department store at the mall.

"You must be Cale. So, how did you meet Julius? Are you in the class for dumb kids, too?"

Cale raised his eyebrows and looked at JT nervously. It was the first time he'd ever heard JT called Julius, and it was the first time he'd ever heard a parent insult their own kid.

"Offer him some cereal, at least," she said to JT. "Jeez, what an idiot."

"Do you want any cereal?" JT asked quietly.

Cale felt too stunned even to sit at the table. He shook his head, wanting to leave as quickly as possible.

"You don't say much, do you?" said JT's mom. With that, she got up, walked inside the trailer, and began to rummage around loudly.

JT looked away, but not before Cale saw the look on his face, like a scolded dog. Cale stared at the cereal and milk sitting on the worn picnic table and thought about what he could say to JT. Everything he thought of seemed insulting to his mom.

A moment later, JT's mom bolted from the trailer, speaking loudly on her cell phone. She opened the gate and then slammed it shut. The gate had squeaked loudly, and Cale then realized that was why they'd taken the shortcut under the fence last night.

"Normally, she's alright," JT said. "I think she's having a fight with her boyfriend, that's all. Sure you don't want any breakfast?" JT's voice sounded perfectly normal.

"Nah, I gotta go," Cale said, as he grabbed his board. "I guess I'll see you later."

Cale couldn't get home fast enough. He couldn't believe how mean JT's mom had been. When he reached his house, he felt completely exhausted. He trudged up the stairs, dropped his board on the porch, and pushed the door open.

"Mom?" Cale's voice cracked. "Mom, please tell me you're home."

Cale's mom walked up the stairs from the basement and poked her head out of the doorway. She took one look at Cale and walked over to him with her arms open. He squeezed her tight.

"I'm really sorry, Mom," he said, feeling safe in her warm embrace.

Cale told his mom everything. Well, almost everything — he didn't tell her about the police car crash. He did tell his mom that he'd gone to the big city the night before instead of just to

JT's and told her about how they got there. That seemed to be the thing that freaked her out the most. "Riding in the back of a pickup truck is a really good way to die," she said. "One good bump and you could have been thrown under the wheels of another car."

Cale was surprised by what she said next.

"You know," she said, "I might have even let you go downtown with Mark and the guys if you'd asked — as long as you wore a *seatbelt.*"

Cale perked up when she said this but she quickly dashed his hopes.

"But not anymore, Cale. It's going to take me a long time to *fully* trust you again."

Finally, Cale told his mom about JT's home life. Cale's mom sat and listened, and at the end of his story, she sat silently for a while.

"I wish I could give some parents a shake. There is no reason to treat your children like that, no matter how bad things get. And JT's such an interesting kid." Cale felt better for getting it off his chest, but he still felt awful for JT. "Mom, do you think we could, just, uh, let him stay here if things ever got bad at his place? Only like a night or two?"

Cale's mom didn't hesitate before answering. "Anytime, Cale. You tell him he can come here anytime."

"There's one more thing," Cale said. "I'm entering the contest this Saturday. Can you come and watch?" As soon as he'd asked, he felt his feet and his jaw tense. He couldn't believe he'd just said the words out loud. And by asking his mom to come, he'd really committed himself. For a wild moment, he hoped his mother would ground him or something, so he couldn't go after all.

No such luck. His mom beamed. "Looking forward to it!" she said.

★   ★   ★

That night, Cale spent a long time awake and staring at his ceiling. He felt nervous about the contest, which was only two days away. He wondered what tricks he was going to do on what obstacles, and then his thoughts drifted back to the night before. He remembered how great it felt to land that backside one-eighty kickflip in front of Mark. Then he thought about how lost in the city JT and he would have been if the pickup hadn't found them when it did. *I would have been fine if we had a map*, he thought.

He sprang from his bed and cleared off his desk. He got out his map-drawing supplies and set to work. He was going to draw the map he'd imagined the night before. First he checked his hand-drawn map of Drayton to make sure he got King's Court right from overhead, and then he tried his best to remember every obstacle and to draw them in perfectly. He drew the quarterpipes, the pyramid, the flat bars and handrails. He even drew the houses on the street and the mini-ramp in Toby's backyard. Finally, he drew a few cars in the driveways of the street. By the time he was done, he felt much calmer. He went back to bed and was asleep in a minute.

CHAPTER 8
THE MENTAL POSSE

The next day at the plaza, the guys started talking about the contest, and it made Cale shake with excitement. He had told himself that he wanted to enter the contest, and he'd told his mom. But he hadn't told the guys. For some reason, he felt that as soon as he told them, it would make things that much more official.

"I may not even enter it," JT said. "I don't get why it's such a big deal to see who's better, or whatever," he added. Cale couldn't believe his ears. JT was the best skater of the crew, and here he was turning down an opportunity to show all of Drayton his skills, not to mention make a hundred bucks or so in prize money — not a bad paycheque for a day's skating. But instead of urging JT to enter, all Cale could do was kick a few little rocks around and pretend he wasn't listening.

"You've gotta enter it, man. I'm entering. We should all enter," Skylar said, "to represent the Seven Stair Crew."

JT thought this over for a few moments, tick-tacking his board around the plaza. "You gonna enter it, Cale?" JT asked, fishing for some kind of reaction.

Cale didn't know what to say to JT. Cale wanted to say yes, but he also wanted to act cool, like it wasn't a big deal. Instead of answering, Cale pulled out the map he'd drawn the night before and laid it on the concrete bench he was sitting on.

"I drew a sketch of the competition area," he said, unfolding the sheet of graph paper. He was worried at first that they would think he was a geek, but as they eagerly approached, his worries disappeared.

"Did you draw that?" Josh asked.

"Yup," said Cale.

"It's amazing," Josh said, lifting off his hat and scratching his head.

"Just think of all the lines you could do!" Skylar said, drawing a route with his fingers across the page. "You could start here, do a big trick over the box ... then, like, slide this rail here ... then go up this quarter-pipe and get some speed, then air over the whole box!"

Cale watched JT's eyes drift around the map, his brow knit in concentration.

"You're right. You could actually ollie over the whole box and slide or grind that handrail on the far side!" JT said, his voice filled with excitement. He grabbed Cale by the shoulder, never even lifting his eyes off the page. "This drawing is amazing, man."

The guys talked for almost an hour, planning lines, talking about tricks and about who would be at the contest. It was getting late. Josh had a basketball game to go to and Skylar had to leave for dinner. They all agreed that regardless of whether they were going to enter, they would meet Saturday morning on Josh's driveway at nine, because he lived closest to King's Court.

JT and Cale stayed at the plaza until the sun began to set. Cale stood at the top of the Seven Stairs and thought about how he was going to have to conquer them again once Ryan got home.

"Man, it sucks that the battery died," Cale said. "I don't know if I have it in me to ollie these again."

"I wouldn't worry about it too much, man. You did it already," JT said, smiling. He then popped into a smooth backside lipslide on the small hubba and hopped off, rolling past Cale, who was confused. JT was the one who set the rules about the stairs. Was he changing them now?

"I would enter the contest, you know," JT said,

"but it costs, like, eight bucks. There's no way I'd ask my mom. I know she can't afford it right now." There was an honesty in JT's voice that told Cale he wasn't looking for a handout.

"I'll lend you the eight bucks, man. You're going to win anyway. You can just pay me back with all the cash you make," Cale said, as if it was already fact.

JT smiled and picked at some splinters flaking off the nose of his board. "I'll only borrow the money from you if you enter the contest, too."

"Deal," Cale said, feeling as if he'd just stepped off a cliff.

"Deal," JT said, putting out his fist for a bump from Cale.

★　　★　　★

The day before the contest, Cale was on his street, skating the little section of waxed curb in front of his house. Josh showed up on his way to the plaza and joined Cale with a few slides on the curb. After a few minutes of goofing around on the little obstacle, they decided to head into town and check out the plaza. They knew Ryan was going to return from his trip soon and it was the most beautiful day of spring break so far.

They sped into town, cracking big ollies over

everything in sight. To Cale, that was one of the best parts of skateboarding — just cruising around, doing big ollies over manhole covers, up curbs, down little steps, or over whatever he passed.

When they got close to the plaza, they saw a kid they didn't recognize pop a huge backside one-eighty ollie down the Seven Stairs in front of them. They stopped their skateboards and watched from afar.

"Who is that?" Josh said, his eyes narrowing.

Josh and Cale could hear the yelling and whooping of what sounded like a dozen kids hanging out in the plaza — their plaza.

"Maybe it's JT with some of the guys from Douglas High?" Cale said hopefully. But somehow, he knew that these guys were intruders and doubted that JT was among them. Sure enough, a minute later, JT and Skylar rolled up behind Josh and Cale.

"What's up?" Skylar asked. "What's going on?"

"I dunno," said Josh. "Some other kids are skating our spot."

JT kept rolling past and peered up the Seven, where the noises of skateboards and voices echoed around. JT looked back at the rest of the crew. He signalled them to join him. The guys hopped off their boards and ran to catch up with JT, who was now bounding up the Seven Stairs toward the unknown skaters.

As the rest of the crew followed JT, they heard glass break. Shivers of adrenaline shot up Cale's back. Whoever was skating on the turf of the Seven Stair Crew didn't sound like they were giving it much respect.

Skylar, Cale, and Josh rounded the corner to see JT standing defiantly at the edge of the four stairs near the centre of the square. In front of him were at least five guys probably about fifteen years old. Cale didn't recognize any of them as local Drayton skaters, and it was hard to tell them apart. They were all wearing black hoodies and black jeans, almost like it was their uniform. Cale could see a smashed bottle right at the bottom of the small hubba, shattered into dozens of pieces that sparkled in the sun. It was right in the hubba's landing zone.

"You guys gonna clean that up?" JT asked, sliding his board back and forth under his left foot.

A few of the guys in black whipped their heads up as the tallest one of them rolled up to JT. He pulled his hood off, revealing a shock of black dyed hair.

"You own this place, kid?" he sneered.

"Oooh!" mocked the gang in black in chorus. One of them even slapped the nose of his board on the ground like some monkey wanting to see some action.

JT didn't budge and kept his head up, looking at their leader as he floated by. "It's right in the landing, dude. Clean it up," he snapped.

Cale was by far the youngest in the plaza and he felt so small and exposed that he took a step sideways, so he was behind Josh. He tried not to make it too obvious he was hiding.

"Who are you guys?" said another of the rival guys, perhaps second in command.

"We're the Seven Stair Crew," Skylar said, stepping forward. "And this is where we skate. Every day," he added for effect.

The tall leader snickered. "What? Did your mom come up with that name?" he said. "You know where *I* skate every day?" He didn't wait for an answer. "Wherever the hell I want!"

"We wouldn't smash bottles on the ground at any skate spot. It's just stupid," Josh said, his voice booming in a way that Cale had never heard.

"Just clean it up, dude," JT said, trying to end the standoff.

"Why don't *you* clean it up, you little grom," the leader said.

"I'll bet he skates way better than you, buddy," Skylar said.

This got the leader's attention. He turned his head and spat on the ground. "Is that right? Here's the deal, you little scrapes. I'll play a game of S-K-A-T-E with shrimpy here," he said, pointing at JT, "and whoever loses cleans up the glass."

Another chorus of whoops and jeers rose from the kids in all black.

JT, cool as ever, took off his plaid shirt and tossed it on one of the benches. "Whatever you say, man. Can we use the benches?" he asked politely, almost mocking his opponent.

"Use whatever obstacles you want, grommet," he said. "I'll still kick your butt."

The game of S-K-A-T-E was just like the basketball game H-O-R-S-E but instead of shooting baskets, skaters attempted to out-trick each other. If the first player landed the trick, the second player had to follow up with a reasonable version of the same trick. If he couldn't pull off the trick, he got a letter. Once one of the players racked up enough letters to spell *skate*, he lost.

"Losers go first," JT said with a smile. *Smart*, thought Cale. Going first would give the tall kid a bit of an advantage but also give JT a chance to check out his skill level.

"Rip it up, Jer!" one of the tall kid's friends called out. It was the first time they'd put a name to their leader.

Jer rolled up his sleeves as he rolled toward one

of the flat ledges. He snapped a low but controlled pop shove-it and did a fifty-fifty grind on the edge with ease.

Jer was goofy-footed, which meant that JT had to come at the obstacle the other way — which he did, but with a bit too much speed. He popped the shove-it well but the trucks stuck on the ledge and JT bailed, rolling on the ground on his back.

He popped himself back up as the kids in black jeered out, "S. You got an S, man."

Jer spun his board under his palm, thinking up his next trick. He turned to his second-in-command and high-fived. "Tweeze, man, this is going to be even easier than I thought."

The mood in the place had grown serious. On one set of benches, the kids in black stood elbowing each other for the best view. Across the way on another bench stood the Seven Stair Crew, plus Cale, worried that JT was down a letter.

Jer rolled casually on the flat ground, opting not to use an obstacle this time. He popped a huge nollie heelflip, catching it on unscuffed black skate shoes before landing on his board's bolts and rolling away, knees bent.

JT, taking his time, drifted out into the open before popping an equally impressive heelflip into the air. But before he could land, one of the kids in black yelped loudly. It messed with JT's concentration and his board flew out of his control. He put his hands out and looked in the direction of the yeller.

"What's that for, buddy?" JT exclaimed. "That's so uncool."

"K!" yelled the kids in black, giving each other high-fives and ignoring JT.

JT took a deep breath and turned back to Jer, who was setting up for his next trick.

"You wachin' this, kid?" Jer asked. It was so quiet that Rudy, the guy who worked at the sandwich shop, peeked his head outside to see what was going on in the plaza.

Jer rolled parallel to one of the benches and nollied up onto it. He lost control of his board, which went flying like a twisted, bouncing spring. It came to a rest as it hit one of the walls of the plaza.

Now it was JT's turn for control of the game. He started out simple, with a frontside heelflip varial, not going for pop, just to stomp the landing.

Jer was unable to follow up with his own version, his board skidding out of control upside down.

"S," Josh said, matter-of-factly. Jer gave the Seven Stair Crew the evil eye.

"Right on, JT, right on," Skylar said, ignoring him.

It was JT's turn again, and this time, his upped the ante with a successful double kickflip, then rode away calmly.

The next few minutes were a flat-ground battle between the two competitors. They were fairly evenly matched, and they would flip-flop between being in control and playing catch-up. Crazy tricks were thrown down: JT did a nollie three-sixty flip that Jer was unable to do. Then Jer would do something that JT couldn't convert, like a backside late shove-it or a backside bigspin to fakie nosegrind on one of the benches.

Both JT and Jer had S-K-A-T when Jer, in control, decided to do something totally cheap. He rolled toward the hubba, the side without the glass at the bottom, and popped a simple fifty-fifty grind down it. His guys cheered and hollered, as JT looked at him with confusion.

"There's glass at the bottom of my landing. Even if I land it, I'll slam into the glass," he said.

"Then clean up the glass! You're going to have to anyway!" Jer said, his crew nodding in agreement.

Cale jumped down from his perch on the bench and grabbed a piece of cardboard from the trash. He walked toward the pile of glass shards.

"Cale," JT said, "don't even think about it."

Cale backed away. He hopped back up on the

bench, not quite understanding what JT planned to do.

Without hesitation, JT rolled at the hubba switch and fifty-fiftied the whole thing going the opposite way, landing on the side free of glass. A roar came from the Seven Stair Crew's bench and a smile came to JT's face.

By the look on Jer's face, Cale could tell he was in shock that JT had made it. Jer set up for a hard-flip on flat but mistimed his ollie and messed up the trick.

"What were you trying there?" JT asked, like he was friends with his opponent.

"Hardflip," Jer said, breathing hard.

"Oh," JT said. "Ever tried one down a set of seven stairs?" But JT wasn't looking for an answer from Jer. He was calling out his next move.

Skylar and Josh ran the long run-up toward the Seven Stairs and perched themselves on the bench with the best view. Thinking quickly, Cale followed them and hustled down the steps to act as a lookout. The kids in black had perched them-selves on the opposite side of the run-up, standing on a bench a bit further back. It wasn't as good a view, but they could still see whether or not JT made the trick.

Cale saw that all was clear and he gave Josh

a wave. Josh nodded at JT, and JT took off. He cranked three huge pushes, got low, judged his speed and then took another big push, setting up his feet for the trick. His deck popped off the ground with a crack and arced through the air with the impossible twist of a hardflip. He twisted his body and lifted his legs over the board that drifted below him and then rose to his feet like magic. He cradled the nose with his front foot as the back bolts met with the sole of his back foot. He landed with a smooth smack and rolled away perfectly.

JT had hardflipped the seven!

Cheers went up from both sides of the run-up. Even the kids in black were amazed at what JT had just accomplished.

All eyes turned to Jer, who was rolling toward the Seven Stairs with almost no speed. Stepping off his board, he clicked his tongue, acting too cool to even try it.

By now, the sun had dipped behind the clouds and the day turned dark. It looked like it might rain. Jer signalled to his crew to follow him down the stairs away from the plaza.

"Hey, buddy, if you don't try the trick, you lose by default," Skylar called out.

Jer ignored him, instead calling out to JT across

the street. "I didn't say anything about using the stairs, grommet."

"Go clean up the glass," Josh said with authority.

"Forget that," Jer said, pulling his hood over his head.

"Clean it yourself," said Tweeze.

"We gotta be somewhere," Jer said, snapping his head to signal the others to follow him.

As they began to walk away from the plaza, Tweeze snatched Cale's board and pretended to throw it.

"Give me my board back!" Cale yelled.

"What are you gonna do? Tell on me?" Tweeze laughed.

"Just give him his board back, you sore losers!" Josh yelled.

With this comment, Tweeze went into a rage. "Who the hell are you talking to, you little turd!" he screamed.

Jer stepped in front of Tweeze. "Listen, you little pieces of dirt, if you're thinkin' about going to the contest at King's Court, you better be ready for a serious beating. From the Mental Posse!" He grabbed Cale's deck from Tweeze, threw it down, and then raised one of his big feet in the air. He stomped in the middle of the deck and snapped the new board in two.

"See you around, grommets," Jer said, tucking his hands into his sleeves and skating away with the rest of the Mental Posse rolling like a fleet of black warships behind him.

CHAPTER 9
PART OF THE CREW

Cale fought back tears as he kicked the ground in front of him. He had saved up money by countless shovels-full of snow only to have his board turned into a heap of kindling by a bunch of jerks. He bit his lip to stop it quivering as he went to pick up his broken board. He grabbed the two ends by their trucks, the whole thing still sort of sticking together with a weak membrane of grip tape.

Little droplets of rain started to dot the sidewalk and the guys ran for cover in the plaza. Cale turned his ball cap around backwards before climbing the Seven Stairs, so that a few of the raindrops would hit his face, disguising the tears that had begun to drip down his cheeks. He didn't want his friends to see him cry, so he kept his head turned away from them as they ducked under one of the overhangs in the plaza.

"That sucks, man," Josh said to him as Cale sat down on a bench with his skateboard across his lap.

Skylar leaned in and surveyed the damage. "That guy is such a knob, man," he said.

JT was rolling through the dry parts of the plaza, still charged from the S-K-A-T-E game. "Cale," he called from the far corner. "Now you *have* to go in the competition tomorrow. You're way better than most of those guys."

Cale knew that even if JT was right, the Mental Posse were older and now capable of instilling such fear that Cale would be too intimidated to land a single trick.

"And we'll be right beside you, man. We'll make sure they don't mess with you again," Josh said, as he looked at Skylar and JT, who both nodded in support.

"Yeah, you're one of us," Skylar said.

"But what am I going to skate on?" Cale asked.

At that moment, Ryan stepped into the plaza, his shoulders spotted with raindrops. He was walking with crutches, sporting a huge smile, a sunburned nose, and an air-cast on his leg.

"What did I miss?" Ryan asked.

The guys filled Ryan in on everything — the contest, JT and Cale's trip downtown, and the Mental Posse and JT's amazing win. "More importantly, what the heck happened to you?" Josh asked.

"Put it this way," Ryan said proudly, "don't ever do backflips into the shallow end of a hotel pool. Not even if you're making cute girls from Kansas laugh," he added. "It's not worth it."

The guys started to laugh. Having Ryan back felt like a beam of sunlight on a day that had turned rainy and cold. Cale stood up and bumped fists with Ryan.

"Welcome back, man, it's good to see you," Cale said.

Then he remembered. He looked down at his broken board, then back to Ryan.

"I ollied the Seven," Cale said matter-of-factly.

"'Atta boy! Welcome to the crew!" Ry said, grabbing Cale in a pretend headlock that ground Cale's face into one of his crutches.

"Thanks," Cale said. "But since you weren't here, it didn't count."

"C'mon! Forget that. If you did it, you did it. I didn't need to be there." Ry looked to the rest of the crew for agreement, and everybody turned to JT.

"Listen," said JT. "Tomorrow, before the contest, we'll meet at Josh's. That way, we'll show up at the contest together, as *one* crew. All of us. That means Cale, too."

Did this mean Cale was officially part of the crew, or not?

Cale was thankful that they would roll to the contest together, at least. The last thing he wanted to do was show up alone.

★   ★   ★

When Cale got home, he hid his snapped board in a dark corner of his garage. He faked a smile all through dinner, and although he thought about telling his mom what had happened to him and his skateboard, he didn't. Cale's mom was pretty protective of him and he wanted to deal with the Mental Posse himself, with the SSC. Whatever his status with the crew may be, he knew they had his back.

Cale went to bed earlier than normal. He wanted to have a good sleep so he'd be ready for the next day. As he lay in bed, his mind jumped from one thought to another. Images and sounds of the Mental Posse flashed in his head: he saw their sour faces, heard the echo of their intimidating laughs. It drove him crazy. He sat up in bed and gritted his teeth.

Stop it! he mentally snapped at himself, trying to control his thoughts. *This is exactly how they want you to feel.*

He took a few calming breaths and flipped the fear on its back. *They think they're so great! Wait till they see what the Seven Stair Crew can do! We owned the plaza, and we'll own the contest, too. 'Cause we're the real street kings!*

Holding victory in his mind, Cale lay down again, breathing slowly and steadily. At last, he dropped off.

★   ★   ★

Cale woke up to his mom shaking him. He glanced at his little alarm clock, which was flashing *12:00, 12:00, 12:00.*

"I wasn't sure what time the contest was so I thought I'd better wake you," said Mom. "The power went out last night."

"What time is it?" he asked sleepily.

"Almost nine."

"It's okay. The contest doesn't start until eleven," said Cale, yawning. Then he remembered that the crew was meeting at Josh's at nine.

"Can you make me some toast?" he asked his mom, then raced to get dressed.

"What's the rush?" Mom asked when Cale got to the kitchen. Cale didn't answer. He just grabbed his toast, pulled on his striped hooded sweatshirt and ran down the steps of his house toward Josh's. He had forgotten how slow things were when not on a skateboard. He thought of the distance he had to go and the fact that he was already late. He turned around, ran back up his driveway, and crashed through the front door of his house.

"He's back!" his mom said, trying to be funny.

"Mom, I need a ride to Josh's," he said. "Please?"

She flipped a page of the paper and lifted her head.

"Please, Mom, please, I'm already late," he pleaded.

She smiled. "Get in the car, mister."

On the way, thoughts raced through his mind. *What if they'd already left? How can I ride without a board? Do I go to the contest alone?* He could barely keep still.

His mom rounded the final corner and turned down Josh's street. Cale could see Josh's driveway, which looked empty as they drove toward it. Cale craned his neck to see if maybe they were on Josh's front porch. Nobody there. Cale's mom slowed to a stop at the bottom of the driveway.

"Mom, do you think you could wait?" Cale asked. "Just to make sure that they're here."

He didn't wait for her to answer. He hopped from the car and ran toward Josh's dark-green front door. He banged on it twice and pressed the door-bell at the same time.

Nothing. No sound of footsteps coming to the door; not a voice calling from inside; nothing. He looked back at his mom in the car, patiently waiting.

He held up his finger, pleading with his eyes that he needed one more minute. Cale ran through a gate and down the side of the house to the back-yard, where he could see Josh's dad, fiddling with a whipper snipper's blade.

"Mr. McGavin!" Cale called to him. "Mr. McGavin!"

Mr. McGavin lifted his head, looked around, caught sight of Cale, and took the little yellow ear-plugs out of his ears. "They're in the basement," he said.

Cale ran back out front to wave to his mom. "Thanks, Mom! See you at the contest!"

Mom beckoned him closer. "Where's your skateboard, mister?" she called. "Don't you think you'll need that today?"

"Long story!" Cale called back, and she drove away.

Cale walked up to the door and let himself into the house quietly. He removed his skate shoes and set them neatly beside all the other skate shoes of the Seven Stair Crew. Slinking down the stairs into the finished basement, he could hear the guys talking in hushed tones. He heard his name mentioned. Rounding the corner, he could see all of them, watching something on the TV.

"Press STOP," JT said, turning to look at Cale. "Hey man, what's up?"

The rest of the guys were sitting on a big couch, except for Josh, who was lying on the floor, manning the video camera that was hooked up to the TV. The guys looked like they were hiding something from Cale and it annoyed him. They were all smiling, like they had just heard the punchline to some great joke that Cale had missed out on.

"What are you guys watching?" Cale asked. "What's so funny?" His stomach whirled around with nervousness.

"Have a seat," Ryan said, sliding his crutches off the big leather couch, allowing room for Cale to sit down.

Cale didn't budge. He just stood in the room and looked at Josh. "Josh, what's going on? Why are you guys acting so weird?"

"Just sit down, man," Josh said reassuringly. "We've got something to show you."

He pressed play and the video started to roll: Cale pushing rapidly toward the Seven Stairs, his wheels spinning loudly on the pavement; Cale setting up for the ollie and snapping it; Cale clearing the long stairs as if he'd done it a million times before.

"But I thought . . ." Cale couldn't believe what he'd just seen.

"You thought what?" JT said. "You thought we'd tell you that you were in the crew before Ry saw the footage? Yeah, right!"

The guys laughed and a weight lifted from Cale's shoulders. They hadn't been making fun of him or talking smack behind his back. They'd been showing Ryan the footage — the footage that Josh had told Cale didn't exist.

"So, Josh, you were lying when you said the battery ran out?" Cale asked.

"Yup, I hated to do it, but JT's right, man, Ry had to see it first," Josh explained.

Cale smiled and shook his head.

"Welcome to the Seven Stair Crew!" Skylar said, jumping on Cale's back, which triggered a big pile-on with all the guys on top of Cale.

"Get off, get off," Cale laughed, his lungs crushed by his attackers.

"You're entering the contest, buddy. Crew orders," said JT, climbing off the pile of bodies. "You'll borrow Ry's board until you get enough money to buy a new one."

Cale smiled as he straightened out his clothes. It sunk in a bit that he was now part of the crew, and it filled him with a sense of belonging.

Josh looked at his watch as he began to put away the old video equipment. "We should go."

CHAPTER 10
CONTEST JITTERS

The Seven Stair Crew rolled along Sir William Avenue with JT in front as usual, followed by Skylar, then Josh, then Cale, who was piloting Ry's board with Ryan sitting on it, holding his crutches across his lap and using them for balance. As they got closer to King's Court, they noticed cars parked on both sides of all the streets surrounding the cul-de-sac where the competition was going to take place.

JT turned around to the rest of the guys. "Wow, it's really busy," he said. To add to the energy of the day, there was a PA system playing music, interrupted by announcements.

As they got even closer, they could see the entrance to King's Court knotted up with bystanders and a few parents in Day-Glo safety vests. JT dismounted his board, picked it up, and snaked his way through the crowds that were forming. The rest of the guys did the same, except for Cale, who kept rolling Ry forward through the crowd on the skateboard.

"Excuse me, injured dude comin' through! Injured skater coming through!" Ryan announced to everybody.

People smiled and gave way as Cale rolled Ryan closer to the competition area. They got a clear view of the street section of the course: the small wooden barricades, the bright flag tape, the spectators. There must have been more than a hundred people there, and almost as many skaters. The big difference was a huge digital time clock that sat beside a pop-up canopy overtop of the judges' table.

Cale could see Russ standing beside the canopy, wearing shades and holding a couple of sheets of paper, a bottle of water, and a microphone.

"If you haven't picked up your entry forms, please do so now," Russ was saying. "We're going to start the thirteen-and-under division in ten minutes, followed by fourteen-to-sixteen, and then Masters, which is anyone over sixteen."

Cale thought this was a bit funny. Weren't "Masters" old dudes who golfed? "Let's see if Toby has a chair for you," said Cale, rolling Ry toward the judges' table. He could see Toby under the tent, wearing a goofy hat and handing out entry forms.

"Hey, Toby, do you think Ry could grab a chair from you guys?" Cale asked.

"Sure, if he doesn't mind being the timekeeper," Toby replied, too busy to look up.

"Yeah, I'll do it," said Ry. "Where do I sit?"

"Huh? Well, we need all of these spots for the judges, so you'll have to sit in this," Toby said, standing up and grabbing a folding lawn chair from under the table. He unfolded it and placed it beside the huge time clock.

Cale helped Ry off the skateboard and onto the lawn chair, which was frayed on a few of the waxy plaid straps. Russ walked over and began to show Ry how to use the START, STOP, and RESET buttons on the stopwatch.

"You sign in yet?" Russ asked Cale.

"Nope," Cale replied, walking to the judges' table and grabbing a form from Toby.

Josh and Skylar were filling out their forms on the underside of their boards. JT used Josh's back as a sort of desk.

"Hey, Cale, can I talk to you for a second, man?"

JT pulled Cale over and whispered into his ear, "Is it still cool if I, uh, borrow that money?"

"Sure," Cale said, reaching into his pocket and pulling out two rumpled tens.

"Hey, don't make it so obvious, dude," JT said,

dropping his arms to the side and looking over his shoulder.

"Here's that ten bucks I owe you, man," Cale said, the volume of his voice increasing. "Now we're square."

JT looked earnestly at Cale and took the bill from his hand. "Thanks," he said.

They had a bunch of stuff to fill out on the entry forms, like their names, birthdays, and what kind of skateboard they were riding. Cale checked to see what kind of board he had borrowed from Ry. He spun the graphic side toward him, but it was too covered with stickers to tell. On that part of the form, he just wrote "borrowed." He didn't know why the judges needed that information anyway.

"Are you entering the mini-ramp contest?" JT asked.

"No. You?"

"Nah, I think I'll stick to street," JT said, as he checked the box beside *Street Course (best run of two)*.

They made their way to the practice session. Everyone from all age groups wanted a chance to hit the obstacles as many times as they could before the contest started. Some skaters started by dropping in on one of the quarter-pipes at either end, then hitting the obstacles, while other skaters would just run with their boards when they saw an open opportunity and try to pop in a trick or two.

Cale tried to find an opening in the swarms of skaters as they zipped past, hit an obstacle, then either slammed or landed their tricks, before getting out of the way of the next skater. Cale thought the course looked like a conveyor belt of skateboarders. If a skater landed a trick over the box or down one of the handrails, the spectators would cheer and clap. If the skater fell, there was no reaction from the crowd. However, if a skater took a crazy bail, the audience would let out a sizzling chorus of "Ooooh!" It was almost like people had come to witness the wild bails as much as they had come for the great skating.

Cale finally felt a lull. He ran with his board toward the big box, planning on just snapping a quick backside ollie over the hip to get his bearings. He saw something out of the corner of his eye at the last second. Another skater had dropped in on the far quarter-pipe and was lined up to hit the opposite side of the same object. Cale jumped off his board before he hit the ramp. If he had ollied, he and this other skater, a guy called Raz, would have collided mid-air.

"Watch it," Raz said, as he toed a weak ollie over the hip and rolled past Cale.

Although it wasn't his fault, Cale felt a wave of

humiliation. Which brought up something he hadn't remembered until now: the Mental Posse. Were they even here? He hadn't seen them, but there were so many skaters, and more arriving every second. His question was answered when he grabbed his board and climbed to the top of the big quarter-pipe at the east end of the obstacles. Up on the deck of the ramp, he had a full view of the world around him, and looking out toward the entrance of King's Court, he could see Jer, Tweeze, and the rest of the Mental Posse drifting in like a flock of dark birds.

Cale's stomach sank as the Mental Posse pushed through the crowd toward the judges' table. They hadn't seen him yet, but by the way they scanned the crowd, he felt like they were looking for him or any of the Seven Stair Crew.

There was still practice time left and Cale hadn't hit any obstacles. He decided he'd better, if he wanted to get his mind off the Mental Posse and into the contest.

Picking his moment, Cale dropped into the six-foot transition of the quarter-pipe, which gave him enough speed to carry right to the hip he'd attempted to hit before. Just before he went for the backside ollie he'd planned, a *backside one-eighty flip* popped into his head. Before he knew it, he was sailing through the air with the board rotating below him in a controlled single rotation. He sucked up his legs as the board came to meet his feet, turned his shoulders at the last second, and felt the wheels of his board land smoothly on the Masonite. A surge of excitement rippled up through him as the crowd cheered.

"Nice one, Cale," Josh said as Cale rolled toward his friends, feeling safe standing beside the crew to which he now belonged. Cale lifted the hem of his bright yellow T-shirt and wiped the sweat off his brow.

"You see who showed up?" Cale said to JT and Josh as Skylar ripped away, seeing an opening on the pyramid.

"No, who?" Then, realizing who Cale must be referring to, he said in a mocking voice, "Let me guess, the Mental Posse."

Josh peered over the crowd on tiptoes, trying to spot them. "Don't worry about them. Just concentrate on your own runs. You do that and you'll win our age group, no problem," he encouraged, before skating away toward the low flatbar and feeble-grinding it perfectly.

Cale scoped the crowd again. This time, he didn't see any of the members of the Mental Posse, but he did see someone who put the pressure on even more: Angie. She was standing on a set of stairs beside Sarah's driveway, which gave her a good vantage point for the contest. She wasn't paying any attention to the rest of the skaters, just standing on the concrete steps with her back against the bricks of the house, staring directly at Cale. They locked eyes and held each other's gaze for a few moments, before Sarah walked outside with two plastic glasses and a pitcher of fruit punch. Cale looked at the ground, his heartbeat increasing and his palms beginning to sweat.

"Please clear the course. The thirteen-and-under contest is about to begin. Please clear the course," Russ said, hushing the crowd a bit.

Russ read out the names of the first heat of young skaters, which included Josh, Skylar, and a dozen other skaters, but not Cale.

Good, Cale thought. *I have some time.* He pulled the crumpled map of the course from his pocket. Now it was much more than just a map; it had notes and arrows and names of tricks to try. It was, in short, his game plan.

He watched Skylar's runs, which included a lot of good technical tricks, like a three-sixty flip and a nollie flip five-o grind, both of which were landed smoothly. But his line lacked any high ollies or grab tricks. The other thing Cale noticed was that Skylar ignored the quarter-pipes altogether, choosing to run with his board between tricks and never trying a lip trick on their big metal copings. He bailed a couple of times, too. A half-cab heelflip over the hip messed him up, and when he tried a little shove-it thing on the pyramid, he lost his momentum and his confidence. His board spun out of control as the one-minute timer buzzed, signifying the end of his run. Skylar was pretty stoked, though — the judges advanced him to the final round.

Russ had explained that three riders from each of the two heats would advance to the finals and that there would be prize money for the top three in the finals and prizes for the top six. That meant if you made it into the finals, you'd win something, even if it was just a T-shirt or a couple of stickers from Drayton Skates.

Josh's runs were alright, too, though he seemed to be lacking technical tricks the way Skylar lacked in hitting the big stuff. Josh did a massive ollie-to-tail over the hip and a backside five-o on one of the big quarter-pipes. He also nose-slid the hubba and did a backside lipslide on the small rail. He popped a huge Indy grab over the whole box but slammed when he hit the pavement on the far side. He also fell every time he tried a flip trick; even a kickflip on flat gave him trouble. But the crowd seemed to be into his big ollies and cheered even louder than they had for Skylar.

For some reason the judges weren't into Josh's run and when Russ announced the three skaters that would be advancing, Josh wasn't on the list. That meant the best he could do was fourth place. Russ began announcing the second heat, and Cale was relieved when he heard his name boom out of the speakers. He took a deep breath. He had seen the Mental Posse yip and holler when Russ called the name "Jason Cruz," letting Cale know he was going to have to skate against one of *them*.

Jason Cruz was a really good skater. He tore across the obstacles with a lot of speed and control. His best tricks were the nollie flip he did over the hip and the switch five-o grind he did down the rail. As Cale watched him, he knew that Jason Cruz would be the one to beat.

"Cale Finch," Russ's voice boomed. "You're next. One minute on the clock, please. The time begins as soon as you step on your board."

Cale felt rushed as he was getting set at the top of the quarter-pipe. He could see his mom wearing a big pair of sunglasses and a puffy linen blouse. She was standing near the judges' table, and when she saw that Cale had picked her out, she called to him.

"Knock 'em dead, honey!" she yelled.

"Knock 'em dead, honey!" one of the guys in

the Mental Posse echoed, mocking Cale's mom and making Cale even more nervous.

Cale smiled awkwardly at his mom, then took a quick look to see if Angie was watching. He couldn't see her. Looking down to where he'd been sitting with the Seven Stair Crew, he saw no one. He felt incredibly small at the top of the big ramp.

"Check out the poser with his borrowed board!" Tweeze yelled, making the Mental Posse practically double over with shrill laughter.

Cale wished he were somewhere else. Anywhere but here. As if the contest itself wasn't nerve-racking enough, he had the Mental Posse making fun of him, he couldn't see his crew, and he was forgetting his tricks and his line. Cale had major butterflies in his stomach as Russ urged him to begin.

Before he was feeling fully ready, Cale dropped in on the quarter-pipe. He was leaning a bit too far back as he rode down the transition, and at the bottom of the ramp, he dragged his tail and lost his balance. He didn't fall off his board but he might as well have. He had lost all his speed and had to deviate from hitting the hip. Instead, he rolled toward the low flat slider-bar, but it was a horrible start to his first run.

Cale popped a low one-eighty ollie and set up for a trick on the low square metal bar. He snapped a fakie ollie, hardly hitting his tail, and locked into a fakie nosegrind on the lowest part of the rail. He came off the grind sketchy and had to kick his tail and turn his body around. He had landed the trick, but it was not what he had planned at all.

Cale rolled up the quarter-pipe at the other end of the course and got a bit more speed as he set up for a trick on the small pyramid. He popped a nollie flip on the flat and landed it, which got the crowd going. He readied himself for a pop shove-it over the pyramid. He was so stiff and nervous that he felt like he was trapped in someone else's body, someone who was thinking too much, afraid to bail and afraid to give the course his all.

Cale messed up his ollie at the top of the pyramid and lost control of his board. It went spinning toward the crowd. As he ran to get it, he took a quick glance at the big red numbers on the clock. He had only fifteen seconds left. He looked around the course and his mind went blank. He couldn't think of a single trick to try. With the time winding down, he ran up on top of the big box and, feeling defeated, tried to boardslide the hubba. He had given up. Feeling like he didn't have enough speed and not feeling like the trick even mattered anyway, he jumped off his board, picked it up and ran to the sidelines to sit down beside the first person he recognized: Josh.

"Let's hear it for Cale Finch, everybody," Russ said, dragging a few claps and whistles from the crowd, which was less than stoked at Cale's run.

"How'd your run go?" Josh asked, taking a big bite of his mustard-slathered hotdog.

"I feel like such a loser," Cale replied, pulling his T-shirt up over his face.

"Sorry we missed it, man. The lineup at the barbeque was really long," Josh said.

"It was the worst. I sucked," Cale said.

"What happened?" Josh said, wiping his mouth with a paper napkin.

"Forget this, I'm leaving. This is stupid," Cale said, standing up and beginning to walk into the crowd.

Josh called something to Cale as he disappeared into the crowd, his face still covered by his T-shirt. Josh's mouth was full of hotdog, so not much of a sound came out. Cale bobbed though the crowd. Someone passing tugged him on the arm. It was JT.

"Cale, where are you going?" he asked.

"Home," Cale replied, shaking loose from JT's grip and feeling the shudder of tears begin in his face. He kept walking.

JT caught up with him where the crowd became more sparse.

"What's wrong with you, man?" JT said.

"I'm outta here. This whole contest was a bad idea. I'm not cut out to be a street king." Cale said, his throat choked.

"Hey, buddy, I don't even know what a street king is. That was just something to get people's attention on the flyer. You're part of the SSC, man, that's what matters!" JT said. The hotdog he was holding began to drip globs of mustard and ketchup onto the grass.

Cale stormed off, away from the contest area, and down the cement pathway that led to the schoolyard nearby. He was too angry to listen to JT, too angry to think about the Seven Stair Crew, too angry even to think about his second run. He just wanted to get as far away from everything as possible.

CHAPTER 11
MARK'S WISDOM

Cale could still hear the noise from the contest drifting over the schoolyard as he sat on the stairs behind one of the portables and took in deep, shaky breaths. Part of him wished he'd never set foot on a skateboard. It was the one thing he loved most — the thing he lived for, and now it just felt so pointless.

His head snapped up when he heard a set of skate wheels rolling somewhere nearby. He stood up, grabbed his skateboard, and bounded down the steps. He turned his back to the noise of the skateboard and began running in the direction of his house.

"Hey, Cale, wait up!" a familiar voice called out. It made Cale stop and spin around.

Mark Skinner was rolling casually toward Cale, drinking a can of Coke and holding another can in his other hand. "Want a Coke, dude?" Mark asked, rolling right up to Cale and sliding the cold can into his hand.

"Tell me what's goin' on buddy," Mark said.

Cale sat down, cracked his can open, and took a sip of the Coke. It felt really good going down his throat.

"I missed your first run, man, sorry. Your mom said you looked disappointed," Mark said.

Cale didn't even know where to start, so he said nothing. Mark sat down on his skateboard, too. "It's a lot of pressure, isn't it?" Mark said.

Cale nodded.

"I'm gonna tell you a story, Cale, about a local skater who, when he was your age, had trouble competing in a contest," Mark said. "He was an amazing skater, real stylish and everything, and everybody knew it. One day, the skate park in Drayton — this was back when Drayton had one — put on a contest. Everybody knew this kid was good and they expected him to win the contest. Anyway, the contest rolled around and the kid was almost too nervous to enter, but all his friends were telling him he had to enter and everything. So he did. And guess what happened?"

Cale took another sip of his Coke and answered, "He won?"

"No!" Mark said, laughing. "He was horrible. It was like watching a different kid skate altogether. He had no style; he kept falling; it was a disaster. He tried so hard that it did him in. He was used to skateboarding because it was fun. It usually made him feel great and now it just made him nervous. So he decided to stop trying so hard and just skate for himself. He would knock out all the distractions around him and just skate like he was having fun, goofing around, you know? And you know what happened?"

"He never won a contest ever, right?" Cale said.

"No, Cale, he started to win them. He just tried to please himself, by thinking about why he stepped on a board in the first place: for fun."

Mark stood up. "Here's the deal, Cale. You take your second run and pretend there aren't two hundred people there. Pretend you're just skating with your dudes and there's no one else in the whole place. Sound good?" Mark reached out his hand and pulled Cale to his feet. "Remember that trick you landed downtown in front of me the other night?" he asked, smiling. "That's the confident Cale I want to see out there."

"Yeah, but what about those Mental Posse guys?" Cale said, remembering that they were still there.

"Whattaya mean?" Mark asked.

"They were saying all kinds of stuff before I dropped in. They psyched me out," Cale explained.

"What did I say?" Mark said.

"I know, I know, pretend they're not there," Cale said.

The two of them walked back to the contest, where Cale could hear Russ's voice announcing Josh's name. The second runs were about to start. As they got really close to the edge of the crowd, Mark held out his hand for Cale to slap. Cale gave him five.

"Have a good run, dude. Think of something that makes you feel good and then step on your board and just have fun. Be confident — because you *rip!*" Mark said, walking toward the crowd to get a better view of the course.

Cale called after him, "Hey, Mark. That kid you were telling me about. It's *you,* right? I mean, you're the kid in the story."

"I'll tell you some other time," Mark said, and walked into the madness of the King's Court crowd.

CHAPTER 12
STREET KINGS

Cale pulled out his map of the course again and studied it. He thought of tricks and lines, and created not only a plan A, but also a plan B, in case he messed up.

When Cale heard Russ call his name, he ran out of the crowd with his board and jumped onto it. Cale cleared his mind, just as Mark had suggested, and the noise of the crowd settled and eventually disappeared. Then, mentally, Cale did the same thing with every other distraction: he pushed the Mental Posse, his mom, Angie, and even Ryan and the big digital timer into the back of his mind.

He pictured the map in his head again and pushed quickly across the smooth asphalt, then casually snapped a three-sixty kickflip that floated beautifully in the air. He grabbed it on his feet and smoothly landed, just like he'd do on the flatground of the plaza.

He then zipped toward the hip and popped a frontside one-eighty heel nicely over it. He rolled to the quarter-pipe and rolled up it fakie, then pumped once for speed. He rolled toward the pyramid and spun a low but very smooth backside three-sixty ollie, which he landed easily. He had landed every trick without even trying. In fact, he even had a smile on his face. Mark was right.

Cale decided to hit one last obstacle before he ended his run. Rolling with speed toward the big box, he went up the flat bank fakie and switch-ollied the hubba. The crowd went crazy. Cale looked at the clock — three seconds left. Just for fun, he kicked a frontside one-eighty no-comply, which he landed, and then rolled up to his friends.

Then he snapped back into reality.

The crew was jumping up and down, hugging Cale and cheering his name proudly.

Cale just stood there and took it all in: the crowd clapping, his crew surrounding him. It gave him goosebumps.

"I just did it like I was skating at the plaza," he said to the guys, nonchalantly.

"Yeah, well, I never saw you land a three-sixty ollie before!" JT said.

They turned toward the judges, who were tallying their scores. Every judge, except for Frank (who ran the local bike shop) gave Cale a 9.5. Frank gave Cale a 10.

"I don't want to jinx things," Russ said over the speakers, "but I think Cale Finch will be the one to watch in the finals!"

"Did you hear that, bro?" Skylar said. "You're going to be in the finals, too!" Cale had missed it, but both Skylar and Josh had completed amazing second runs, and all three of them would be in the finals.

Russ announced just seconds later, "The following skaters from this heat will move on to the finals: Skylar Petersen, Jason Cruz, and Cale Finch. Please report to the judges' table." At the judges' table, Russ told the guys they'd each get one run. Their best two runs from the day would determine the winner.

Cale thought about this. His second run had been near-perfect but his first run was a wash. He had to put in a good final run.

So did Skylar. But Jason Cruz, who had nailed two solid runs already, could use this final round to try crazy tricks and tougher lines.

Skylar went first and put in a pretty good run, landing most of his tricks but messing up when he tried to do a nose-manual down the hubba. Even though he had fifteen seconds left, Skylar raised his board in the air as a "thank you" to the crowd and limped to the sidelines. The crowd cheered and clapped quietly, like they'd just witnessed a good putt by a golfer.

"My ankle is jacked, I think," Skylar said. "I need some ice." The paramedics came to his aid, snapping a chemical ice pack into service and laying it on Skylar's ankle.

Josh was dropping in on the quarter-pipe at this time and he looked really nervous.

"You're gonna have to win this for us," Skylar said, leaning his head back in pain.

"He will," JT said with confidence.

Cale sat on the ground, taking deep breaths to ready himself. Just skating for fun seemed impossible now, with the crowd seeming to swell with anticipation. It fell silent, waiting for him.

Cale jogged from his spot beside JT and Skylar, climbed the quarter pipe, and looked down at the crowd. He saw Ry sitting beside the huge clock, which was set with a giant red 01:00. He nudged his board close to the lip of the ramp, lifted his tail, and extended the deck over the edge. He popped his back truck up over the coping and leaned on his tail, snapping his wheels into place like a piece of Lego. He scanned the crowd, felt the hot sun in his face, and let out a slow breath. "You are a member of the Seven Stair Crew," he said to himself, letting the sense of accomplishment and belonging wash over him. It made him so proud. All of a sudden, the crowd disappeared, and Cale's mind calmed. "Just have fun," he said to himself.

Placing his front foot over his bolts, he dug his rear foot into the grip tape. He transferred his weight and plunged his front foot downward on the board as he dropped in. His stomach see-sawed as he flew down the transition and rolled rapidly toward the big hip.

Backside flip, he said to himself as he reached the top of the flat bank of the hip, cracking, then kicking, a spinning backside ollie, just like he'd done in practice. This time, though, he wasn't as lucky and the deck got away from him a bit. He was able to land it but his right foot dragged a bit, slowing him down. He was sure the trick came off as sketchy but he didn't care. It felt good. He approached the low square metal flatbar and drifted a half-cab to boardslide, coming off smooth and setting him up on the right line for the quarter-pipe at the opposite end of the course. He kicked a high turn almost at the coping and zipped down the ramp toward the jump-ramp side of the funbox beside the handrail. He ollied a huge pop shove-it, which carried him almost all the way over the funbox to where he'd begun. He rolled up the quarter-pipe with speed and locked into a pivot on his rear truck, stalling for a brief moment before rolling down the transition fakie and approaching the pyramid. Even with the insulation of his own thoughts, he could hear the crowd roar as he came away from the quarter-pipe.

Cale was setting up his feet for a switch frontside bigspin over the pyramid when he looked at the clock. He had twenty-five seconds left.

That's when he realized his shoe was untied.

He popped a huge switch frontside bigspin over the pyramid and landed it beautifully, but the shoelace of his front foot became tangled in his front wheels. Instead of panicking about a faceplant, he calmly leaned onto his tail and came to a stop. He looked up in the sky and saw a dark bird drifting above him. It snapped him back to reality.

"Twenty seconds, Cale," Russ said as the crowd began screaming and clapping. A few voices seemed to be telling Russ to stop the clock.

Cale tried to stay relaxed, untangling his shoelace from the place where it had become jammed between his wheel and his truck's axle. He heard Angie's calling, "You've still got time! You've still got time!" Her cute raspy voice cut through the rest of the crowd.

Cale tied his shoe tightly and picked up his

board. "I've got nothing more to lose now," Cale said to himself, convinced the clock was about to stop with his run only half-completed. "Might as have fun with it."

He began to push with his right leg as hard as he could toward the quarter-pipe where he'd started. He planned to get as much speed as possible to try a trick over the big box.

His mind raced as he zipped to the top of the ramp and snapped into a fifty-fifty stall. He mentally flipped through trick ideas that he had written on his home-drawn map, then his mind flung itself back to something Skylar had said in the plaza a few days ago.

"You could air over the whole box!" Skylar's words echoed softly but clearly in memory.

Cale stalled on his trucks for what seemed like forever before dropping back in and taking three huge pushes toward the big box. Totally ignoring the clock, Cale bumped up the ramp with more speed than any skater had used yet and cracked a huge ollie over the box. His eyes were aimed directly at the big handrail that slid down the end of the box. That's where he was headed. He piloted his board through the air, which stuck to his feet like it was Velcroed on.

What happened next blew everyone away. Cale landed on the rail in a perfect backside smith grind that he slid on the very end of the rail. As he neared the end of the black metal bar, he leaned on his tail, ollied a little, and landed on the asphalt as the timer clicked from :02, to :01, and then to :00.

The crowd went crazy. Cale found himself surrounded by the Seven Stair Crew and many others. They jumped up and down around him, making him feel like he was in the centre of the mosh pit at a punk-rock concert.

"That was insane!" JT yelled out in the mayhem.

"Sickest trick ever," Skylar added.

"That's our boy, that's our boy!" shouted out Josh.

Everything cooled down as Cale walked to the sidelines, his friends following, roughing up his hair. Russ made the announcement.

"Alright, it's just going to take a few moments for the judges to tabulate the scores, so just sit tight."

After several minutes, Russ's voice boomed over the cul-de-sac. "Alright, skaters, after some heavy deliberation, we have our final decisions.

"In fourth place, Josh McGavin, taking home a nice REWL T-shirt and some new bearings from Drayton Skates Skateshop," Russ said into the mike, like a game-show host. "In third place, winning thirty dollars and a Drayton Skates long-sleeve T-shirt, Skylar Peterson."

Cale's heart thumped loudly in his chest and he held his breath. How great would it be to win, after everything he'd been through?

"In second place, winning eighty dollars and a bag full of so much stuff I can hardly lift it," Russ continued, his voice ricocheting around the crowd and the ramps, "Cale Finch."

Cale let out his breath and quickly followed Skylar who was on his way to the tent to pick up his prize. When he arrived at the tent, Mark leaned in toward Cale and shook his hand.

"Everybody's saying you should have got first, man," Mark said. "And think about it, you weren't even trying. You were just having fun."

Cale remembered the last part of his final run and felt a rush shoot through his body. He had been so sure he'd lost that he had dared the best trick ever.

"I would have taken second if I was able to skate, man!" A voice called out behind Cale. It was Ryan, still sitting in the chair beside the big timer, had a huge smile on his face. "Not a bad showing for the SSC — second, third, and fourth!" he said. "I can't wait til JT gets a chance to skate in the next heat. He'll take first for sure!"

Ryan was right. JT did win his age group. He not only took top prize but beat Tweeze in the same heat, which gave Cale a measure of satisfaction. Standing with the guys in his crew, cheering JT on to first place, gave Cale a surge of confidence and feeling of belonging he'd never experienced before. Cale felt like he would remember this day forever.

And it didn't quit.

As Cale was helping clean up King's Court after the contest, he heard the unmistakable raspy voice of Angie. Somehow, she'd walked right up beside him without him even noticing.

"You were so amazing today," she said. "I think you should have won."

Cale looked at the ground, trying not to act excited. But his heart was thumping like crazy. Just being close to Angie made him feel amazing.

"I never thought I'd even enter the contest," Cale said, "but I'm actually really glad I did."

Angie held out a small spiral notebook and a pink pen. "Will you sign this for me?"

Cale rolled his eyes. "Are you serious?" He said, acting like he thought the request was crazy. But he took the pen and notebook.

"You can also write your phone number if you want to. But, uh, only if you want to," she said.

Cale's hand was shaking, but he managed to scratch out his home phone number on the lined page.

"Maybe you can teach me some of those tricks?" she said.

"Only if you teach me how to shoot hoops," Cale replied, wondering if he'd said too much.

"Hey, loverboy!" Ryan called out. "I gotta get home for dinner."

Cale smiled a little embarrassed smirk, gave a tiny wave, and walked away. As he rolled Ryan home, he was giddy with excitement. It was almost like he'd forgotten about the contest. All he could think about was Angie.

"You can keep my board for a while," Ryan said, as Cale opened the door to his house for him. "After all, I know where you live!"

"Thanks," Cale said. "I'll probably get a new one in the next few days anyway." He thought about his prize winnings and the big bag of swag that his mom had taken home for him.

Cale rolled back toward his house, but before he turned onto his street, he aimed his board for the centre of town. He wasn't sure why, but he was heading toward the Seven Stairs. He popped a frontside one-eighty over a sewer grate, and then floated a half-cab over another. He felt attached to his skateboard like never before, like it was a part of him. In fact, as Cale looked into the pink horizon where the clouds lined up like a set of wispy stairs into the distance, he felt connected to everything.

He snapped an ollie up the curb that led into the plaza. A lone figure sat on one of the benches in the shadows. As Cale got closer and his eyes adjusted in the dying light, he could see it was JT. He looked ticked.

"You alright, man?" Cale asked, stopping his board with a heel.

"Fine. I'm fine. It's just . . ." JT took a long inhale and gathered his thoughts. "It's my mom. I went home after the contest. I was so proud. I mean . . ." He stopped, then continued as if something were stuck in his throat. "She's always complaining about money, so I gave her the hundred bucks I won. I thought she'd be happy. Instead she told me I should get a job, not waste my time rolling around on 'a useless piece of junk.' That's what she called it. 'A useless piece of junk.' Whatever. I took off. Her boyfriend was there, anyway."

"That sucks, man," said Cale, for once sure about what to say. "Hey, wanna crash at my place tonight? It's been such a great day, I kinda don't want it to end, you know?"

JT sat silently on the bench, sliding his skateboard back and forth under his feet, like he was weighing his options.

"So, how about it?" Cale said, trying to be casual.

"Sure, man," JT said. "That sounds good."

JT popped up from the bench, threw his board on the ground, and jumped on it. As he rolled slowly toward the street, he wiped his eyes with the bottom of his T-shirt.

Cale waited a bit, to give him space, then threw down his board and gave it a little push to catch up. They rolled north, toward the part of Drayton's Main Street where the asphalt tilted into a small hill. They started to pick up speed at they reached the top of the pitch. Cale flexed his legs to avoid speed-wobbles and felt a surge of energy as his board picked up speed.

He spun his head and locked eyes with JT, who was backlit by the glow of the buildings and streetlights, a look of sheer joy on his face. At that moment, Cale understood exactly what it meant to be a street king.

Cale spun back around and felt the wind whip by his face. From somewhere deep inside his body, he felt an almost uncontrollable impulse, and without thinking, he let out a loud, wild scream of joy, and the echo hung in the spring air for a few long seconds.